SPOTLIGHT ON LOVE

"There's a fantastic double feature at the Carnegie this weekend," David said. "Would you like to go?"

Callie looked at David, who was grinning shyly down at her. "I'd love to," she replied breathlessly.

David's face lit up. "Great! How about Friday? I'll pick you up at seven-thirty."

All summer she'd hardly dared to talk to him. But she had dreamed of this moment over and over. In her imagination she was sophisticated and confident. She pictured herself casually accepting, as if popular guys asked her out every day of the week. Now that it was really happening, all that confidence disappeared. But Callie didn't mind—she was deliriously happy.

"I can't think of a better way to celebrate, can you?"

"Celebrate what?" Callie asked.

"The new star of the Kennedy High musical!" Dave cleared his throat. "Ladies and gentlemen, let me introduce America's newest stage sensation, Miss Callie Lloyd!"

Bantam Sweet Dreams Romances
Ask your bookseller for the books you have missed

Spotlight On Love

Nancy Pines

BANTAM BOOKS
TORONTO • NEW YORK • LONDON • SYDNEY

RL 5, IL age 11 and up

SPOTLIGHT ON LOVE
A Bantam Book / February 1984

Cover photo by Pat Hill

ISBN 0-553-23964-3

Published simultaneously in the United States and Canada

PRINTED IN THE UNITED STATES OF AMERICA

O   0 9 8 7 6 5 4 3 2 1

To
the Coach and the Bear,
and to those who know who they are

Chapter One

"Callie! Callie, over here!"

Callie Lloyd saw Julia Dougherty waving to her across the Commons of Kennedy High. As Callie pushed her way through the throng of students milling around before homeroom, she noticed the usual crew from the drama club surrounding Julia. Mike Selak and Richie Sanders were talking to Angela DiMarco and Cathy Hoffman. And, as usual, Howie Jensen was standing nearby, trying to look as if he belonged. Callie scanned the group again, searching for one face in particular, but without success.

"I just have a minute," yelled Callie. "I haven't been to my locker yet. Ye olde rickety school bus was late again this morning," Callie explained, approaching her friends.

1

"Where's your better half?" asked Mike Selak. He meant Jennifer Harmon, his girlfriend and Callie's best friend. Jennifer and Callie had been friends since fourth grade and were inseparable, except, of course, when Jennifer was with Mike.

"She went to the library," Callie replied.

"Women!" Mike said and groaned. "I shall *die* from lack of attention."

"Let me know when you expire, Frogman, so I can inherit your Walkman and your goggles," Callie said, joking. Everyone laughed. Mike had just made the swim team and now was rarely seen without a pair of goggles around his neck and small orange disks over his ears.

"Wow, Callie, I still can't get over how terrific you look compared to last year. You'll have to tell me your secret," Julia said coyly.

"No secret, Jule. Just a lot of willpower and hard work."

Over the summer Callie had lost thirty pounds. In addition to a strict diet, she had swum fifty laps at the local pool every day. The only compensation for her grueling routine had been watching the flab disappear. When she looked in the mirror now, she couldn't believe her eyes. For the first time in her life, she was *not* a butterball. In fact, when she slipped into a brand-new pair of tight designer jeans, with her medium-length brown hair and bright blue eyes, Callie was really pleased with the way she looked.

"Well, I bet it will make a big difference come auditions," Julia said. "Did you see the posters? We're doing *Guys and Dolls* this year. Tryouts are on Wednesday."

"How could I forget, Julia. *I* was the one who stayed after school to put those posters up!"

Every year Kennedy High put on a musical extravangaza. The drama coach selected a Broadway classic, which was performed for three consecutive nights at school, and some of the top songs were sung a week before the performances, at Rosedale Nursing Home. The musical was the biggest event of the year for the kids in the drama club, and now that she was a junior, Callie was longing to play the lead.

She had always been in plays—in school or at camp—for as long as she could remember, but she had always played a character part— the "funny girl" or the "fat girl"—like the year before when she was Bloody Mary in *South Pacific*. But this year was going to be different. Callie had struggled all summer to lose the weight so she could get a serious part. She wanted to play the romantic lead, the one the leading guy fell in love with. "No more funny girl parts for me," she had repeated to herself as she swam up and down the pool every day.

A group of students pushed by her, and Callie studied their faces, hoping to catch a glimpse of that curly hair she could spot from a mile away. *Where is he?* Callie wondered to herself, sighing softly.

"Only a couple of minutes till the bell," Callie finally said. "I'd better get to my locker. See all you guys later."

As she walked away, she heard Mike call, "Hey, Dave, how's it going?"

Now he shows up! Callie muttered to herself. David Palmer was a senior who had gotten the lead in every musical since he had entered Kennedy High. He was tall and good-looking, with dark hair, deep-set blue eyes, and an easy smile. Callie had seen him all summer long at the community pool where she had done her laps. Dave was a lifeguard there, and although they smiled at each other, they hadn't really had a conversation since they were in *South Pacific* together. As the summer wore on, Callie found herself hoping more and more that David would notice her, but he never said much more than hello. Now that school had begun and the big musical was just around the corner, Callie had started dreaming about playing opposite him in the show.

As she hurried to her locker, she felt like kicking herself for not hanging out in the Commons just two minutes longer that morning.

Callie's fourth-period class was American literature, taught by Ken Morgan, the drama coach. As she walked into class, she heard him call her from the front of the room.

After she got to his desk, he said "Callie, I need someone responsible to do a job for me."

"What did you have in mind, Chief?" Ken was the youngest member of the faculty at Kennedy, and everyone felt at ease with him. He encouraged students to regard him as a friend and told them to call him by his first name.

"You know that every year we put on a little performance at the Rosedale Nursing Home. Well, I need someone to go over there and speak to the director about this year's arrangements. Are you free after school today?"

Callie bit her lip. She didn't want to tell Ken that she and Jennifer had planned to spend the afternoon rehearsing for the auditions.

"Uh, not today, Ken. I have something urgent to do. How about tomorrow?"

"Mr. Stern is expecting somebody today. I think he's leaving on a business trip tomorrow. I know this is really short notice. Maybe I can find somebody else."

Callie didn't want to let Ken down right before auditions. "I have lunch fifth period, and then I have study hall. The nursing home isn't far away. If you write me a pass, I'm sure I can do it during that time."

"You don't mind giving up lunch and your study period?"

Callie shook her head.

"Great! I knew I could count on you. Speak to me after class, and I'll fill you in on the details."

Callie munched her sandwich as she made her way over to Rosedale Nursing Home. She was disappointed about skipping lunch in the cafeteria with the drama kids because David Palmer was sure to be there. But right now, keeping Ken happy was most important. She wanted to get the part of Sarah Brown, the lead in *Guys and Dolls*. It meant more to her than anything, and if she did get the part, she and David would have plenty of time to spend together.

They had both been in *South Pacific*, but Emile de Becque and Bloody Mary didn't have a real scene together. And there had been so many people around all the time, what with everyone in the chorus and the orchestra, that they had hardly ever gotten to talk. Plus, David was dating Karen Archer at the time. Karen was hard to top! In her three years at Kennedy, she had starred in every musical the school put on. Karen was away at college now, studying to become a professional actress. Callie was hoping David was free to date somebody else.

Talent scores really high with him, Callie thought to herself as she reflected on Karen and David. Karen wasn't the prettiest or even the nicest person Callie had ever met. If only she could get the lead, she would show David that Karen wasn't the only girl around who could sing and dance! And by rehearsing together constantly, getting to know David was—well, inevitable.

Before she realized it, she was at Rosedale Nursing Home. As she walked in the door, she stole a quick glance at the notes she had made while talking to Ken.

"Can I help you, dear?" The woman at the front desk was smiling at Callie.

"My name's Callie Lloyd, from Kennedy High.

I'm here to see Mr. Stern about doing a performance for the residents," Callie said.

"Oh, yes. Mr. Stern is expecting you, but not this early. I believe he has somebody in the office right now, but if you don't mind waiting over there—" she said, pointing to a couch in the lobby.

Callie sat down and looked around. *Everything feels so strange,* she thought. Despite the flowers all around and the colorful paintings on the walls, Callie felt uneasy. The home had the odor of a place that was too clean. It smelled sort of like ammonia or the astringent she used on her face. The cleanliness was stifling. Callie picked up a magazine to take her mind off her surroundings.

"Young lady!"

Startled, Callie looked up to see a wheelchair coming right at her. In it was an old woman wearing a bathrobe. Her white hair fell haphazardly around her face.

"Y-yes? Are you speaking to me?" Callie asked politely.

"No, I'm talking to the Queen of England!" the old woman quipped, delighted at her own joke. "Of course I'm speaking to you. Who are you?"

"My name is Callie. Callie Lloyd."

"There's no one here by the name of Lloyd.

Are you visiting someone?" The old woman peered at her suspiciously.

"No, ma'am. I'm from the high school. I'm here to arrange a show for the residents."

"What kind of show?"

"Every year we put on a musical at Kennedy, and we always come here to do some scenes for the people who can't get to the school."

"Oh, yeah—now I remember. Last year they came and sang some songs from—what was that show?"

"*South Pacific.*"

"That's right, *South Pacific.* Wasn't so hot. I've seen better."

Callie chuckled. The old woman's honesty took her by surprise, but Callie found it amusing—and refreshing.

"Well, ma'am, we *do* try our best."

"Stop calling me ma'am. It makes me feel old. My name's Hattie. Hattie Stevens."

"Well, Mrs. Stevens, I guess we'll have to try even harder this year, with a critic like you in the audience."

"Miss Lloyd, Mr. Stern can see you now," the receptionist interrupted.

"Oh, hush now, Nursie! You're spoiling my fun. Don't you go anywhere, young lady."

"But I have to go now, Mrs. Stevens. Maybe I'll see you again sometime," Callie said.

"When are you coming back?"

"Excuse me?" Callie asked, surprised.

"Are you deaf, child? I said, when are you coming back? We don't get many visitors around here, you know."

"I-I don't know," Callie stammered.

Callie turned to go into Mr. Stern's office. She heard the old woman muttering something about young people today not knowing anything.

When she emerged from her meeting, the receptionist stopped her. "Mrs. Stevens waited for you, but it was time for her lunch. She told me to say goodbye to you."

"Oh, gosh," said Callie. "That's really sweet. She must be lonely. Doesn't anyone come to visit her?"

"No," said the receptionist. "No one that I can think of."

"Doesn't she have any friends here?" Callie asked.

"Not really. She's so gruff, I think she scares most people away. But underneath it all, she's a kindhearted soul. I think she was grateful to have someone to talk to."

Callie left the nursing home and started back to school. She felt sad and confused. She began to wonder what it was like to be old and alone. She couldn't imagine it. Her

10

own grandparents were so different! Her father's parents lived in a community in Florida where they had friends and activities all day. Her mother's parents ran their own business a few towns away, and they still went to work every day. No, she thought to herself, she had never known anyone quite like Hattie Stevens!

Chapter Two

After school that day, Callie stood by the school bus, anxiously searching the crowd for Jennifer Harmon. Finally, a girl with a flash of red hair came hurtling toward the bus. Callie sighed with relief.

"Wow, I thought I was going to miss it," Jennifer said breathlessly.

"What happened this time, Jen? Did you misplace your head? Or lock yourself in the girls' room?" Callie asked, joking with her friend.

"No, I was staring in the mirror, trying to figure out how I could get rid of these freckles!" Jennifer moaned. "When I looked at my watch, I realized the bus was going to leave without me."

"I'm so glad you made it," said Callie as

they climbed on the bus. "We have serious business to attend to."

"You're really determined to get this part, aren't you?" asked Jennifer.

"You *know* I am. Right now it's the most important thing in the world," said Callie. "I want you to help me work up a fantastic number this afternoon, with singing, dancing, and even a little acting. What do you think of the title song from *Cabaret* for the auditions?"

"Wow!" said Jennifer. "That would be terrific. You're really planning to knock 'em dead, eh? What's this part all about, anyway?"

"Well, Sarah Brown is this soul-saving type who works at the Salvation Army. While she's on one of her crusades, she meets this handsome gambler, Sky Masterson. His friends put him up to asking her out on a date! Naturally, a gambler is not the kind of guy Sarah is looking for, but Sky *is* irresistibly suave."

"Fall-on-the-floor gorgeous, right?"

Callie nodded.

"I knew it. What happens to them?"

"*Lots* of things happen to them, but in the end they get married—naturally," Callie replied.

"Isn't it incredible how musicals always have happy endings? Why isn't life like that?"

"I don't know," Callie said thoughtfully.

They fell silent as Callie gazed out the window. Her thoughts returned to Hattie Stevens at the nursing home. *She* didn't seem to be having a happy ending.

I wonder if she's been alone her whole life, Callie mused to herself. *How does someone end up in a place like Rosedale?*

"Is something on your mind?" Jennifer asked, snapping her friend back to reality.

"During lunch today I went over to the nursing home to make the arrangements for our performance there . . ." Callie started.

"I was wondering where you were," Jennifer answered. "How did it go?"

"The arrangements were no problem," Callie said, "but I met the strangest old woman. She was very abrupt—sort of touchy. She gave me the third degree, like I didn't belong there, but then when I told her I had to leave, she didn't want me to go!"

"Sounds creepy to me!" Jennifer said.

"No, she wasn't. In fact, she was sort of sweet in a gruff kind of way. She was funny, too, cackling at her own jokes."

"She sounds like a witch."

Callie knew Jennifer would never understand. She was so lighthearted—she never took herself or anyone else too seriously. Callie looked for a way to change the subject.

"I wonder who will get the part of Sky Masterson," Callie said.

Her friend was incredulous. "When did *you* start losing your brain cells? As long as David Palmer is still at Kennedy, there's not a guy in the school who can hope to get that part!"

"Oh, really?" Callie said, a twinkle in her eye. "Then I guess it will be Dave. Lucky the woman who plays opposite him!"

"I'll say! Now wouldn't *he* be motivation for trying out for the soul-saving Sarah."

"Gee, I guess you're right! I never thought of that!" Callie said, trying to sound innocent.

"*Sure* you never thought of it! Ah, I can see it all now—the future looms before me: I see you. I see Dave. 'Cal-lie, can we run lines? Cal-lie, can we go over that song again? Cal-lie, let's rehearse that kiss a few more times! Cal-lie . . .'"

"Stop!" Callie bopped her friend on the head with a notebook. "Hey! Here's our stop. I'll race you to the front door."

They got off the bus, raced down the sidewalk, then across the front lawn of Callie's house. Her mother was working now, so Callie let herself in. The girls settled in the den and started poking through record albums and the sheet music in the piano bench. Callie's parents were musical buffs, and the had the score to almost every Broadway hit or Hollywood musical there was.

Callie put on the *Guys and Dolls* record so Jennifer could hear a few songs from the show.

"You know," Callie said, "maybe I should audition with a song from *Guys and Dolls* so Ken could get an idea of how wonderful I'll be as Sarah."

"Naw, I heard somewhere that it's tacky to do that. It makes you look too pushy. That's rule number one. Rule number two is *no* ballads," declared Jennifer.

"Why not? Most of Sarah's songs are ballads."

"It's important to audition with something really upbeat—to keep Ken from falling asleep. Don't you remember all those renditions of 'Happy Birthday' last year? I thought Ken was going to die," Jennifer said, laughing. "Let's listen to the song you wanted to do."

Callie pulled out the sound track of *Cabaret* and put it on. Jennifer, who loved the song, got up and started dancing around the room, pretending she had a top hat and cane.

"Wow, what a great idea!" Callie said. She ran to the closet and pulled out one of her father's hats and a long black umbrella. She started to dance next to Jennifer, copying her steps.

The two girls danced around the room, laughing and singing. Finally, Callie stopped and took the record off.

"Come on, Jen. Let's get serious. I need a number to do by Wednesday."

For the next hour and a half, Jennifer worked with Callie, weaving some dancing and some serious acting into the song. By five o'clock, they were exhausted.

"I think we've done enough for one day," Jennifer said wearily. "You've got a terrific number worked up, Cal."

"I couldn't have done it without your help, that's for sure," said Callie gratefully.

"Help, nothing—you're the one with the talent," said Jennifer.

"What are you going to sing for the auditions? Shouldn't we work on a piece for you?" asked Callie.

"Naw, I'm too tired. Besides, it doesn't really matter with me. I'll just end up in the chorus, the way I do every year. I can't sing. Dancing—well, that's another story. I've been dancing all my life! And I've got great legs," Jennifer added, laughing.

"Wait a minute!" said Callie. "I just thought of something."

"What now?"

"Adelaide! There's a great part for you in this play—it's Adelaide. She's the star dancer at a nightclub. She's got this boyfriend, Nathan Detroit, who's also a gambler, and they've been engaged for fourteen years. She spends the whole play trying to get Nathan to marry her, which he finally does in the end."

"So?" said Jennifer.

"So! This part is perfect for you. Adelaide doesn't sing very well, but she's a fabulous dancer. And she's cute and vivacious and spunky—just like you. You'd be a terrific Adelaide!"

"Me? Really? Aw, come on."

"I'm serious, Jen. And Mike is just the person to play Nathan Detroit. I'll bet anything he'll get the role. You and Mike playing Adelaide and Nathan—that's typecasting!"

Jennifer was getting interested. "Does she sing many songs?"

"I'm not sure how many, maybe about four. But you don't have to be Olivia Newton-John. Adelaide is *funny*. She sings through her nose. And she dances a lot. If there's anything you're good at, it's dancing."

"But *me*, a lead?"

"Jen! You know what you're always telling me—'*anything* is possible.' A direct quote."

"Imagine that—little Jenny Harmon playing a main character in the Kennedy High musical. I like the sound of that. And wouldn't it be great if Mike did get to be Nathan?!"

"That's right, Jen. Just think of all those extra rehearsals you could spend with him. Ah, the future looms before me: I see you. I see Mike. 'Je-en, can we run lines? Je-en, let's rehearse that kiss—' "

Jennifer hurled a pillow at her friend, and the two dissolved into laughter.

"There's a scene where Adelaide and Sarah do a song together. That could be you and me!"

"Oh, Callie! It sounds so wonderful! Tomorrow I'll get the script out of the library and read through it. I can just picture it: you playing Sarah opposite David—"

Callie sighed.

"And me playing Adelaide opposite Mike!"

"It couldn't work out any better," Callie agreed.

"I just hope Ken sees things our way," Jennifer said nervously as she began to gather her books.

"Remember, Jen. Anything is possible."

Chapter Three

"OK. Everybody listen up." Julia Dougherty, the stage manager, was standing in the front of the auditorium, clipboard in hand. "If you want to try out for the show, you have to fill out an audition form and hand it in to me. Make sure to fill in everything, *legibly*, and if you use one of our pencils, *return it!*"

"Julia can be such a pain sometimes," Jennifer muttered. Her words were lost on Callie and Mike, who busily scratched away at their questionnaires.

If only I could relax a little, Callie thought as she wrote in the color of her hair. When she came to the question on weight, she proudly filled in "114 pounds," a full thirty pounds less than the year before. She felt a little better.

"All of you who just came to watch can stay, but don't make any noise," Julia bellowed. "Do I have all the forms now?"

Mike dashed up to the stage with their sheets.

"There's nothing to do now but wait," Callie said and sighed.

"I'm in agony. Do you really think I have a chance at the part of Adelaide?" Jennifer pleaded. "Tell me the truth—it makes a difference between going through with this and leaving right now."

"Would you calm down! You're not doing a thing for *my* nerves, either. Of course, I think you have a chance. If I didn't I never would have brought it up."

"Oh, thank you, Callie! I'm so nervous. Are your palms sweating? My palms are sweating. I hope I don't get called first. I want to check out the competition."

Callie was nervous, but she wasn't prone to hysteria as Jennifer was. She was determined to get the part of Sarah and was trying to save every bit of energy for the performance she was about to give. Nothing counted more than this audition. Nothing.

Julia was barking again. "May I have your attention *please*. Thank you. This is the procedure for this afternoon—first, singing auditions, then readings. Dance auditions will be held out in the hall with George, the choreographer, while singing auditions are going on in here. Don't get upset if we stop you halfway through your song. We have a lot of work ahead of us, and we all want to get home at a decent hour. Let's get cracking."

Name after name was called, and one by one people stood in the middle of the vast stage, some bleating, some bellowing, and some singing songs. A couple of sophomores Callie didn't know seemed to be pretty good, but Julia cut them off in the middle of their songs. Jennifer had her turn. She was cute in her pixie way. *But she was right*, Callie thought to herself, *she really can't sing.*

Mike was next, and he was terrific. Then Callie heard her name called. She took a deep breath and walked purposefully to center stage.

On signal, Callie put on her hat, stuck the umbrella under her arm, and went into her routine with all the energy she could muster. She was a little shaky at first, but she could feel herself really getting into it. She danced across the stage and back, and by the time she was belting out her last line, "And I love a cabaret!", everyone in the audience was applauding!

Ken was scribbling notes on her form. Julia shouted, "Thank you! Next up is David Palmer."

Callie was shaking as she walked back to her seat. She sat down and tried to listen as David sang. He did a love song and cast a hushed spell over his audience. Once finished, the quiet broken, Jennifer had a chance to congratulate her friend.

"Cal, you were great!" Jennifer whispered. "I knew you could sing, but I've never heard you sing like *that*. Your 'Bali Ha'i' was sensational last year, of course, but this was so different."

Somehow Callie was more nervous now than she had been before she sang. "Thanks, Jen, but that was the easy part. I'm more worried about the reading."

"How do you think we did?" Mike asked.

"Both of you were terrific. If Ken doesn't give you parts, he's got rocks in his head."

"Hi, guys," came a voice from behind. They turned around to see David Palmer coming up to them.

"Hey, Dave—great audition!" Mike slapped him on the back.

"Thanks. You, too, Frogman," Dave smiled. Mike and Dave were on the swim team together, and this year they seemed to be getting pretty friendly.

Just then Mike and Jennifer were called outside for their dance auditions.

"I think you did a great job, Callie," Dave said sincerely.

David Palmer is complimenting me on my performance. Pull yourself together, Cal.

"Thanks, David." Callie tried to hide her amazement—and the way her heart was racing.

"I knew you could sing, but I never knew you could belt it out like that," he continued. "If I were Ken, I'd put that voice to work where people could hear it. Have you taken lessons?"

Callie's gaze met his. David's eyes were blue, but not icy like some blue eyes. His radiated a warmth that seemed to draw Callie in. Quickly she collected herself, but she could feel the color rising to her cheeks.

"Voice lessons? No, not me." She laughed awkwardly.

"You're really terrific," he said warmly. "You've got a great range."

"Thanks. My dad calls me 'Liza Minnelli of the Showers.' My family's always complaining that they can't shut me up or get into the bathroom!"

Dave laughed, and Callie was relieved.

"Have *you* ever taken voice lessons?" she asked.

"I'd really like to, but I don't have the time right now. I figure when I get to college, I'll have a chance."

"Do you want to major in theater?" Callie asked.

"Theater, literature, biology—you name it. I don't really know what I'm going to major in yet. I love the theater, but it's so tough to make it in show business."

Callie wondered if he had gotten this information firsthand from Karen Archer. Were they writing to each other? Callie's spirits sank.

"I'm also thinking of studying film," Dave continued. "Not to be an actor, though. I like to write, and I might be able to combine those interests and become a critic. Do you like movies?"

"Of course I like movies. Who doesn't?" Callie smiled. "I see a lot of movies two or three times."

"How about old movies, like Hollywood musicals?" David asked, gazing at her intently.

"You mean the ones with all the tap dancing and the water ballets? The kind that are always on TV?" she asked.

He laughed. "That's the kind I mean. Every three weeks one channel or another is guaranteed to be showing *Forty-second Street*."

"I think they're kind of fun," Callie said. "I don't know too much about them, but they're always so happy."

"How would you like to learn a thing or two about the film greats?"

"But there are no film courses at Kennedy."

"That's why you need a private tutor, like me! There's a fantastic double feature at the Carnegie this weekend. It's part of a Fred Astaire-Ginger Rogers festival. That can be your first assignment. Would you like to go?"

Callie looked at David, who was grinning shyly down at her. Before she knew what was happening, her brain went on hold, and her mouth took over.

"On one condition," she said, grinning. "No pop quizzes afterward."

David's face lit up. "Great! How about Friday? I'll pick you up at seven-thirty."

"Terrific!" Callie replied enthusiastically.

All summer she had hardly dared to talk to him. But she had dreamed of this moment over and over. In her imagination she was sophisticated and confident, like Karen Archer. She pictured herself casually accepting his invitation, as if popular guys asked her out every day of the week. Now that it was really happening, all that confidence disappeared, but Callie didn't mind—she was deliriously happy.

"I can't think of a better way to celebrate, can you?" he said, beaming.

"Celebrate what?" Callie asked.

"The new star of the Kennedy High musical!" Dave cleared his throat. "Ladies and gentlemen, let me introduce you to America's newest stage sensation, Miss Callie Lloyd!"

Callie laughed, blushing.

"We don't know that for sure, David. Don't start getting my hopes up."

"Is the lady telling me I don't know talent when I see it?" David asked, faking indignation. He threw back his head and peered through outstretched hands at Callie's face. "Such grace, such talent! Ah, bambina, such eyes." He reached over and pinched Callie's cheeks as he talked in his silly Italian accent.

"We'll just have to see if Ken Morgan concurs with your opinion, Signor Director," Callie added, giggling.

"Fair enough," David replied. "But I'm sure he'll agree."

Callie's hand unconsciously moved to her cheek, where David's warm fingers had been only a moment before. *Can this really be happening? Here's David Palmer, one of the most terrific guys at Kennedy, not only telling me I'm talented but taking me to the movies, too! If I'm dreaming, I don't want to wake up.*

Suddenly all conversation stopped, and all eyes turned to the stage. Someone was singing, and singing beautifully. She was not cut off in the middle as many of the others had been. When she finished, it took Julia a little longer than usual to call the next name. She and Ken were deep in conversation.

Callie didn't recognize the girl who had just sung. "Who was that?" she asked.

"I think her name is Kim, Kim Crawford. She moved in over the summer. Her family lives in our neighborhood."

He seems to know a lot about her, Callie thought nervously. She tried to sound casual. "You know her?"

"I've never met her, but my little brother told me about the new family that moved in."

Julia's booming voice interrupted them.

"OK. Listen up, everybody. David Palmer, Angela DiMarco, Mike Selak, Callie Lloyd, Kim Crawford, Jennifer Harmon"—Julia's voice droned on and on, naming about fifteen people—"will you all please stay. The rest of you can go home. The cast list will be posted on the door of room two thirty-seven Monday morning."

Auditions were in the final stages. Scripts were passed out, and readings for various leads were assigned. When everybody had read at least once, people were mixed and matched, and some read for more than one part. Callie read three times for Sarah and twice for Adelaide. More people were sent home.

Eventually David seemed to be the only one reading for the part of Sky. It was evident to Callie that he had gotten the role. Kim read with him, followed by Callie. Then Kim was called again.

Finally Ken stood up wearily.

"It's been a long day, everyone, but I think I have enough to go on now. Thank you for bearing with me. There are going to be a lot of tough decisions, but I want you to know that you've all done a fine job. Go home and get some grub. David, can you stay a few minutes?"

Callie gathered her things and walked out with Jennifer and Mike.

"I'm so relieved it's all over," Jennifer chattered. "I don't care what happens now—I just don't want to have to go through that ever again!"

As they walked up the block, Callie was

silent. Her mind was swimming with thoughts of David and Kim Crawford.

"Hey, Cal, I think you did a terrific job. You've got the lead for sure," Mike said.

"I don't know, Mike. Kim Crawford is awfully good. It was was so nerve-racking—first her, then me, then her—I felt like I was in a revolving door."

"It seems like it's between you and her for the lead," Jennifer said solemnly. "But I wouldn't worry about it," she added quickly. "She doesn't have your experience—Mike sneaked a look at her questionnaire. And you're just as good as she is, if not better."

"You are, Callie," Mike agreed.

"Thanks, guys. I guess we'll all know on Monday. I don't know why he's making us wait so long. Anyway, when you read for Nathan and Adelaide together, Ken looked absolutely charmed."

Mike grinned.

"Do you really think so, Cal?" Jennifer was getting excited. "I can't wait till the cast list is posted. I know I won't get any sleep until then. Maybe my mother can drive us to school so we can get an early peek."

"Ten minutes won't change fate," Mike said. "We may as well see it when everybody else does."

"I'm with you, Mike. Bad news too early ruins my day," added Callie, laughing nervously.

"Don't be such a pessimist," Jennifer said. "It's obvious that you'll play Sarah, and David"—Jennifer winked—"will be Sky. What were you two talking about when Mike and I went to the dance audition?"

Callie tried to conceal her enthusiasm. "We're just going to the movies Friday night. No big deal."

"How can you be so casual about it?" Jennifer cried. "This is hot news."

Callie broke down. "I can't. I'm really excited!"

"Women!" Mike threw up his hands in mock surrender.

Chapter Four

The rest of the week was excruciating to Callie. She was counting the minutes until Friday night. She didn't know which was worse—not knowing if she got the part of Sarah, or waiting for her date with David. They were both so important!

There was nothing she could do now about the auditions, but her date with David was still an unknown. Both nervous and excited, Callie kept daydreaming about the date. She imagined keeping David laughing with clever remarks, and the two of them having a great time. Then she would panic. *What are we going to talk about all night? How can I ever compare with that dynamite Karen Archer?* It was hard to believe that David had really asked her out. *Me, the fat little butter-*

*ball he saw at the pool all last summer!
Would wonders never cease!*

Friday night finally arrived, and at dinner Callie was unable to eat a thing. *At least I won't get fat before I see him,* she told herself.

"I thought you loved eggplant parmigiana," her father remarked. "When you're not eating, I know something's the matter."

Callie blushed. "Oh, it's nothing, Dad. I'm just having a breakdown over my date with David Palmer. It's nothing—nothing at all!"

"You've got a date with David Palmer?" her brother Hank asked. "*That* David?"

"Yes, *that* David. The gorgeous star of every Kennedy High musical. *That* David!"

"What's the big deal, Cal?" Hank asked sincerely. "Dave's a good guy. I know him from the swim team."

"Did you ever *talk* to him?" Callie asked.

"Of *course*, I talk to him. Who do you think he is—Robert Redford? Come on, he's just a nice guy, and a good swimmer, too."

"That's enough, Hank," Mrs. Lloyd interrupted. "Leave your little sister alone. Between school and auditions and everything else, she has enough on her mind." Callie shot her mother a grateful glance.

When dinner was finally over, Callie raced upstairs. She looked over her wardrobe for the millionth time, trying to decide what to wear. The only new clothes she had bought were jeans and cords. She and her mom had had a big fight about it when they had gone shopping together. Mrs. Lloyd wanted her daughter to "look like a lady" and wear a skirt "every once in a while." Now Callie was a little sorry she hadn't bought more clothes.

What do people wear on dates, anyway? she wondered. She wanted to look really good on her first date with David, but she didn't want to make it obvious that she was trying to impress him. Finally she decided on a pair of olive green cords with a khaki-colored crew neck sweater, over a beige button-down shirt. She got out her loafers and polished them until they looked like new. She checked her watch—Dave would be there to pick her up in ten minutes. Grabbing her brush, she ran to the bathroom.

Callie examined her face carefully. Luckily her skin was clear, but she looked drab now that her summer tan had faded. Cautiously she checked out the brand-new makeup in the medicine cabinet. She had spent two weeks' allowance on it when she was shopping with Julia and Jennifer before school had started. She could just hear Julia's know-it-all words: "Using makeup is the difference between a little girl and a woman." Suddenly she remembered that Karen Archer always wore a lot of makeup. *Well, here goes,* she said to herself.

She opened the mascara and rolled the brush tentatively across her top lashes. After a few strokes, she relaxed a little and applied the mascara to her bottom lashes. She stepped away from the mirror and studied herself. The makeup had worked—her blue eyes seemed larger than they ever had before. "Whew—one down!" she muttered.

"But it's important to put on makeup so it looks like you're not wearing any." Julia had said that, too. Callie decided against using eye shadow and added only a little blusher to her cheeks. Then she heard the doorbell ring. Her stomach did flip-flops.

Quickly Callie brushed her hair as the sound of voices drifted upstairs. Making a part, she secured one side with a tortoiseshell comb. She went into her room and took a last look in the mirror. She really couldn't believe it. She looked slender and graceful—and her face glowed with anticipation.

"Callie," her mother called. "David is here."

Callie grabbed her cotton jacket from her bed and ran to the top of the stairs, where she abruptly stopped and caught her breath.

Casually she walked down the stairs to the living room.

"Hi, David," she said and smiled. David was sitting on the couch, chatting with her father. His eyes widened as he looked at Callie.

"We'd better get going," he said, getting up. "There's sure to be a line. Nice meeting you, Mr. and Mrs. Lloyd."

"Not too late, now," her father said, shaking David's hand. "And make sure you have a dime," he added, grinning.

Outside, David ushered Callie into the front seat of his car.

"What did your father mean about the dime? Hasn't anyone told him that movies have gone up since he was a kid?"

Callie laughed. "Dad always says that. He's not talking about the movies, Dave. He means for a phone call, in case we get into any trouble."

"Trouble? Oh, he must have heard me drive up in this old bomb! I wanted to take my folks' car tonight, but they needed it. We could always get to Main Street by way of Connecticut—that way, no one would see us."

Callie laughed. "That's not necessary. I'll just sit under the seat. Let me know when we get there," she said, faking a dive.

David and Callie were both laughing now,

and Callie's nervousness seemed to dissolve. She knew this was going to be a great evening. It was starting out just right.

Dave reached over and squeezed her hand affectionately.

"Your brother's Hank Lloyd, right?" he asked.

"The one and only! He said you guys are on the swim team together."

"Yup, your brother is one of our top butterfly men. He's a fantastic swimmer."

"He said the same thing about you!" Callie exclaimed.

"No, I just swim to keep in shape. It really keeps me trim. Without my job at the pool and the swim team, you could roll me to the movies!" Dave said, grinning at Callie.

"I know just what you mean. I was at the pool practically every day last summer doing laps,"

"You know, I *thought* I saw you there," David exclaimed. "But I was never sure it was you."

They stopped for a red light.

"Under a bathing cap we all look alike." Callie laughed. "You have the dubious honor, David Palmer, of having seen me at my absolute worst."

"Maybe," he said softly. "But this is most definitely *not* one of those times."

Callie felt a surge of warmth throughout her body. David fumbled with the tape deck as the light changed.

"What would you like to hear?" he asked.

"You choose," she said.

David handed her a tape.

"What's this?" Callie asked.

"Something you'll know inside and out soon enough."

She looked at the cassette case. It was the score from *Guys and Dolls.*

"I brought this tape for you," he explained. "Music is one of my passions. All kinds, especially show music. Have you heard the songs from the show?"

"Some of them. My dad has a fabulous collection of show tunes, and Jennifer and I listened to the album before the auditions."

"Funny, you know, even though Mike and I have become friends, I hardly know Jennifer. You're good friends, aren't you?"

"The best," Callie replied.

"I think we're all going to have a lot of fun doing this show together," David said, smiling at Callie.

"Yes." Shyly Callie looked at David. The sun was just going down, and his profile was beautiful in the fading light. Callie sighed to herself as she thought of how wonderful it would be if she played Sarah opposite his Sky. Not only would they be together all the time, but if they fell in love onstage, maybe—just maybe—it could happen in real life.

They reached the theater in time to grab one of the few remaining parking spaces.

"Let's hurry!" he exclaimed. He took her hand in his, and they ran to the end of the ticket holders' line. "You stay here while I check to see if there are any tickets left."

He let go of Callie's hand and dashed up to the ticket window. He came back smiling, waving two tickets.

"I hear they've been packing the theater every night for this feature. The people in this town obviously have class! There's nothing I like better than a good Fred Astaire-Ginger Rogers flick, and tonight we get to see two of them!" David was so happy, he looked like a kid with a new toy.

But Callie had a joy of her own to keep her occupied, for David had slipped his hand back into hers when he rejoined the line.

As they walked out of the theater, David was bubbling over. "What great movies, huh? I just love that scene where Fred and Ginger are dancing on roller skates." Suddenly David grabbed her around the waist and scooped her up in his arms, twirling her round and round toward the car. The other cars, trying to nose their way out of the parking lot, started to beep their horns at them.

"David!" Callie screamed through her laughter. "You're going to get us killed!"

"Ginger, baby—trust me," he said, placing Callie down on his beat-up Chevy. His grip relaxed, and his hands rested lightly on Callie's arms. He looked tenderly into her eyes and leaned over. He held Callie's face in his hands and kissed her gently on the lips. It was a nice, soft kiss, as romantic as she'd always dreamed it would be. David's lips on hers made her feel beautiful!

"I guess movies like this make me feel romantic," he said softly. "But I have a feeling this would have happened even if we'd gone bowling."

"So do I," Callie said dreamily. "But I hate bowling. The highest score I ever got was a fifty-three," she whispered, looking straight into his eyes.

"I hate bowling, too," he said, "but I like Callie."

He slipped his arms around her as he leaned over again. "There's only one thing I like better than Callie right now," he whispered, "and that's food! C'mon, Ginger. Let's go get a hamburger."

The next morning Callie woke up early and bounded downstairs, where her father was busy fixing breakfast for the family. Her mother, still in her bathrobe, was curled up with the morning paper and a cup of coffee.

"Did you have a nice time last night, dear?" her mother asked, barely stifling a yawn.

"Oh, yes," said Callie. "Fantastic."

"Sure sounds like you had a good time," her father commented, turning some pancakes. "I'm surprised to see you at the table this early. Want some bacon?"

"Whatever's easiest for you, Dad."

"My lord, she *did* have a good time," her mother remarked, putting down her paper. "What did you kids do?"

"First, we went to the Carnegie to see these Fred Astaire-Ginger Rogers movies, which were really great, and then we—"

The phone rang, interrupting Callie's chatter.

"I'll get it," she sang and raced out to the hallway.

Her parents looked at each other, dumbfounded.

"Nine o'clock Saturday morning, yet," her father said, scratching his head. "Maybe we should send her out on dates more often."

"Jennifer, hi! I'm so glad it's you," Callie whispered into the phone. "We had *the* most wonderful time last night. Look out—this *may* be love!"

"You're kidding!" Jennifer screamed. "I knew it. Tell me!"

Callie related every detail of the night before.

"And we're going on a picnic tomorrow, and he's taking me to Moe's after school on Monday!"

Callie hung up, went back into the kitchen, and hugged her mother.

"Mom, you don't have anything for me to do today, do you? Jennifer and I want to go to the mall and check out some of the new fall clothes."

Her mother stared at her. "Why, no, dear, you go right ahead," she said incredulously.

"Well," Callie said, fingering a brown corduroy skirt, "my mother *might* be right. This skirt doesn't look so bad on me."

Jennifer sighed, exasperated. "You look great. When are you going to realize that you aren't *fat* anymore? Here," she said, pushing

45

her friend closer to the mirror, "Callie, I want you to meet Callie. Shake."

Callie laughed. "OK, Jennifer, you win. I don't look like Godzilla."

"So will you take my advice and buy this skirt?"

"I'll have to bring down Mr. and Mrs. Credit Card, but I'm sure they'll be thrilled."

"I know somebody else who's going to be thrilled," Jennifer said teasingly.

"Maybe," Callie said. "But I hope David likes me for other reasons besides my clothes."

"Oh, come off it, Cal. He's not the kind of guy who's taken in by superficial things."

"How do you know?" Callie asked, giggling. "You hardly even know him."

"I just know," Jennifer said earnestly. "Mike wouldn't be his friend if he weren't a good person."

"I don't know, Jen," Callie said with a straight face. "After all, look who Mike goes out with."

"Creep!" Jennifer shouted.

The next day Callie wheeled her bicycle out of the garage and joined David at the end of the driveway. Streaks of white clouds peppered the sky, but the sun's rays shone through, creating a beautiful, warm day. Callie put on her sunglasses.

"Going incognito, Ginger?"

"Wouldn't want to be barraged by fans, you know. Where are you taking me for this feast?"

"That's a secret," he said mysteriously.

They pedaled through Callie's neighborhood until they reached the end of town and the bordering woods. David carefully steered his bicycle onto the path leading into the trees. Callie followed.

"These woods give me the creeps," she shouted after him. "*Where* are we going?"

"Don't worry. You'll be safe."

"Why can't we just go to the state park like everybody else?"

"We're almost there."

Callie sighed and pedaled harder to catch up to him. As they went deeper into the woods, the sun disappeared. Callie took off her sunglasses. Suddenly David stopped and hopped off his bike.

"We'll have to walk the rest of the way. Ready?"

"David, it's dark in here. I don't like it."

"You've never heard of the light at the end of the tunnel? Trust me," he said, resting his hand lightly on her shoulder. "It's worth it."

They made their way silently over the broken branches and soft pine needles. Every now and then the sun peeped through the leaves overhead as squirrels and birds scurried about. Suddenly Callie saw an exquisite clearing up ahead.

"We're here," David said excitedly. "This is my favorite spot in the whole world, I think. I found it when I was a kid."

The soft moss sparkled, and a small brook ran by the edge of the clearing. David spread a blanket on the ground.

"Table for two, madame? Here we have all the amenities of paradise," he said. "Soft lighting, running water, music"—he switched on a transistor radio—"and good home cookin'," he added, laughing.

"Look at all this food." Callie exclaimed as David pulled bundle after bundle from the knapsack. "Who's going to eat all this?"

"Probably *me*. The bottomless pit." He patted his stomach. "But I'm not hungry just yet. Let's get the drinks into the stream so they'll stay cold."

They lay on their stomachs next to the brook. Callie dangled her fingers in the cool water. "I never knew this was here. It's so beautiful."

"Isn't it wonderful?" he replied. "I'm sure other people know about it, but I've never run into anyone here. It's a good thinking spot."

"And what do you think about when you come here?" Callie asked.

"Oh, lots of things. What college will be like. Why I just had a fight with my father. How I'll get through my physics exam. Life. Sometimes I come here to memorize my lines. Right now," he said, turning to her, "I'm thinking about how glad I am you came here with me today."

He brushed a twig from her sweater and ran his fingers through her hair. Silently he leaned over and kissed her.

"Not as glad as I am," Callie breathed. "David, I—"

"Shhh," he whispered.

"I just wanted to say I'm really happy with—with the way things are working out for us."

"That goes double for me, Ginger. Ever since auditions, I've had this feeling about you. I know we don't know each other very well, but—" He paused, searching for the right words. "Let's just say that my instincts about people have never failed me." He grabbed her hand. "Let's eat."

They walked over to the spot where he had left the food. David began opening up packages and setting things out. "We've got sandwiches, chips, fruit—you name it."

Callie, remembering her waistline, picked up an apple and sank her teeth into it.

"How do you like your classes so far?" David asked, popping open a soft-drink can.

"So far, so good. My favorite is Ken's class. I had him last year, too. He makes us read tons of books, but I don't mind. I love to read."

"I had him sophomore year. He was tough, but a lot of fun. What's your schedule?"

"All college prep, basically. Chemistry with Markel, trig with Allison, gym, then Ken's class, lunch the fifth period, study hall the sixth—"

"You eat lunch fifth? So do I. How come I haven't noticed you there?"

"Sometimes I skip lunch. Like this week, I had to run over to Rosedale Nursing Home to set up the performance."

"Really?" David asked with interest.

"It was so weird there. I met a strange old lady. She was funny but sad. She was sort of crusty and hard to get along with, but underneath it all, I think she was desperate for company."

"I guess I can understand that," David said. "My father's mother was in a nursing home. She broke her hip and couldn't take care of herself. We used to visit her all the time until she died. But there were lots of people in the home who never got any visitors. It's really tough on them."

"I guess so. Maybe all those years of loneliness make you bitter. But I kind of like this old lady. There is something warm under that gruff exterior. She is so honest about her feelings and sort of lovable, like Jennifer—only sixty years older," Callie added, giggling.

"Potato chips?" David asked.

"No, thanks."

"The cast list will be up tomorrow morning," David said. "Am I ever *nervous*!"

"*You?* Why? Looks like there's no competition for the male lead."

"You never know," he said solemnly. "I'm hoping so much it hurts."

"I know how you feel," Callie said.

"Let's not talk about it, OK? It's ruining my appetite."

"Deal. Besides," she said, checking her watch, "we'll know in eighteen excruciating hours, anyway."

Eating and laughing and talking, they

stayed in the woods until the sun started to set. When David kissed Callie good night in front of her house that evening, she felt that no matter *how* the play was cast, nothing could ruin her happiness.

Chapter Five

Callie and Jennifer sat side by side on the bus Monday morning in total silence. Each corner they turned brought them closer to school—and the cast list. Finally, the bus pulled into the Kennedy courtyard.

"Well," Jennifer said glumly, "this is it. I'm going to check the list and get it over with."

Callie's heart was pounding. "I don't want to look yet. Why don't you go ahead without me?" she replied, staring straight ahead. "I'll catch up to you later."

Her friend gave her a sympathetic look. "OK. And Callie?"

"Yeah?"

"Good luck."

"Thanks. You, too." She squeezed Jennifer's hand gratefully.

Callie wanted to be alone when she read the list. Slowly, deliberately, she walked to her locker, carefully arranging her books for her morning classes. She hardly noticed the clamor that the students all around her made.

The warning bell rang, and kids began to drift into doorways up and down the hall. *Just three more minutes,* Callie said to herself, *and I'll know what everyone else already knows.*

Those three minutes felt like an eternity, but Callie had to see the list in solitude. She waited until everyone was in homeroom, then made her way to the stairs. As she rounded the corner on the second floor, she watched the room numbers tick by . . . 231, 232 . . . a voice called from behind.

"Callie!" It was Mr. Cole, her history teacher. "I see you're running a little late this morning, so I won't keep you very long."

Callie's heart stopped. "G-good morning, Mr. Cole," she stammered. "How are you?"

"Fine, thank you. I want to ask you something. It'll only take a minute."

Callie thought she'd die! Mr. Cole's brief conversations were exceeded in length only by the encyclopedia.

Callie hardly listened as he rattled on about a class trip to New York City. Even if she were listening, she wouldn't have heard him over the sound of her own heartbeat.

". . . so I was wondering if your mother would care to come along as a chaperon," he concluded.

"My mom's no longer a free-lancer, Mr. Cole. She's working for an agency now."

"Oh!" he exclaimed. "How nice for her! Give her my congratulations, will you?"

"Sure, Mr. Cole," Callie said impatiently. "I'll see you in class." Relieved, she watched him walk away.

When I get there, she thought, *I'll start at the bottom and work my way up the list.* Ken always put the leads at the top and chorus on bottom.

She walked down the hall, to room 237. Still, she didn't look at the list; she looked down at the floor. *Everybody knows but me.* She was trembling.

Slowly she read up the list. Three-quarters of the way through the chorus list up she came to Jennifer's name. She read across.

"Chorus!" Callie cried to herself. She was thankful now that she and Jennifer weren't reading the list together. She couldn't deal with Jennifer's disappointment.

She read farther until she came to Mike's name. "Nathan Detroit." Mike was playing

Nathan opposite somebody other than Jennifer.

Then she saw her own name. Callie held her breath. She read across.

Adelaide.

Callie felt her heart go numb. Quickly she read the last two names: "Sky Masterson—David Palmer. Sarah Brown—Kim Crawford."

Tears collected in her eyes. Instead of getting the lead, she was the *clown* again. And David would be playing opposite Kim!

"Callie, congratulations!" She spun around to see Ken coming toward her.

"You were terrific at auditions," he said jubilantly, "and I'm confident I've got the best little Adelaide this side of the Adirondacks, *including* Broadway."

"Thanks, Ken." Callie fought back the tears. "I tried my best."

Ken didn't notice her disappointment.

"First read-through will be Wednesday after school. Say, can you do me a favor again? There's a problem with the date Mr. Stern suggested, and I need someone to go to Rosedale after school today and get it straightened out. Since you've been on the case since the beginning, I thought—"

After school. Her date with David.

"I'm busy today, but I can go tomorrow, if that's OK."

"Sure. Thanks a lot. I'll give you details after class."

Callie trudged wearily to homeroom, carefully going over every moment of the audition. She thought back to her singing, her dancing. *Maybe I didn't try hard enough*, she thought, berating herself. But she knew she had done her best. *I guess my best isn't good enough.* She thought of Kim Crawford, who had come from nowhere to snatch her most precious dream. Everything inside Callie ached.

Visions of the day ahead flooded her thoughts, and tears welled up again in her eyes. People were going to stop her in the halls to congratulate her, just as Ken had. That awful Julia Dougherty was going to find her and thrust a rehearsal schedule in her hands. She was going to see Jennifer in math.

Jennifer! She had forgotten how awful Jennifer must feel. Hadn't she done the same thing to her best friend that Kim Crawford had done to her? It had to be harder to lose a part to your best friend than to lose it to a total stranger. Jennifer wouldn't have gotten so excited about playing Adelaide if Callie hadn't built up her hopes. *What an awful day this is going to be.*

*　　*　　*

Callie sat in her last class, history, without hearing a word Mr. Cole said. The topic of discussion was the War of 1812, but she was too wrapped up in her own battle to notice. She was miserable about losing the role of Sarah and getting the part her best friend had wanted, especially since it meant she would be playing opposite Jennifer's boyfriend. Callie had wanted to talk to Jennifer after trig, but several kids stopped her to congratulate her on getting Adelaide, and when Callie looked around, Jennifer was gone. Her misery was compounded by her growing anxiety over her date with David. How could she face him in such a wretched mood? *Nobody wants to be around a person who would rather be dead,* she thought ruefully, *and I don't know him well enough to tell him how much the part of Sarah meant to me.*

And that beautiful Kim Crawford! She could never let on how jealous she was of Kim.

Class was over at last, and Callie hurried to her locker. She was to meet David at the student parking lot, and she didn't want to keep him waiting.

Most of all, she thought, *I can't let him see how sorry I'm feeling for myself.*

As she dashed past the gym, images of the day flashed through her mind. At lunchtime Callie had seen Kim Crawford, the Kim Crawford who had been invisible until that morning. She was surrounded by a bunch of kids who had gotten chorus parts. Julia Dougherty was there, fawning all over her.

"I told Ken the *minute* I heard you sing that if he didn't pick you for the part of Sarah, I'd quit the show. I'm glad he had the sense to take my advice," Julia pronounced, full of her own importance. At these words Callie had fled the lunchroom.

Callie arrived at the parking lot, only to find that David hadn't gotten there yet. The last thing she wanted to do was look like she was just standing around waiting for him, so she busied herself by looking over the books cradled in her arms. She spied the script she had hastily stuffed into the pile and sighed. Finally she took it out and started to flip through it. In the front there were descriptions of the various characters.

It said that Adelaide was a cute, lively nightclub star. She had a nasal voice and was known least of all for her brains. But despite her somewhat disreputable career, she was the homey type, with a heart of gold.

Callie was in despair. She looked around for David.

Maybe he's forgotten all about me, she brooded. Now that she was no longer the "new star of the Kennedy High musical," she couldn't blame him. After all, he was used to the lead in Karen Archer, wasn't he? Now the lead was Kim Crawford.

To allay her nerves, she resumed reading. It said that Sarah Brown was tall, beautiful, sweet, and smart.

The star.

"Learning your lines already?" David came up behind her, leaned over, and kissed her. "Ginger, you'll be on Broadway in no time," he said softly. "Did you have a good day?"

He should only know what kind of day I've had. Callie swallowed hard. "You bet! And you?"

"I've been walking on air ever since I saw the cast list," he replied, eyes gleaming. "I'm really excited Ken picked me to play Sky Masterson. I wanted the part so badly. Somebody up there must have heard my prayers."

And nobody heard mine, Callie thought plaintively.

"I've been meaning to congratulate you all day—I guess we just didn't run into each other," she said, trying to make her voice sound bright.

"If we had, I would have given you the biggest whoop and holler I could muster. I'm so proud of you, getting the part of Adelaide. I knew you would." David hugged her closely.

"Thanks," she said, the word almost a whisper.

"You're a natural for a part like that," he stated. "Think of how much you can ham it up. I know you'll have the audience laughing from the minute you walk on stage."

That's the last thing I want, Callie said to herself.

They climbed into David's car.

"You're going to have a great time playing opposite Mike Selak. Old Frogman's the funniest guy I know."

Not as good a time as I would have had playing opposite you.

"Hello?" David said, peering at her. "Are you zoning out on me or something?"

"Sorry," she said quickly, groping for an alibi. "I was just noticing some kids trying to cross the street in the middle of traffic." *Great. Now he thinks an alien has landed in the front seat of his car.*

They drove to Moe's Diner and pulled into the parking lot. Moe's was a down-home place where lots of kids from Kennedy hung out. As David deftly steered Callie to a back booth, she bit her lip and lectured herself. *Get a hold of yourself, Cal—try to forget about the play and concentrate on David and having a good time—or just getting through the afternoon.*

They sat down and looked over the menu. Callie glanced at the table, where people had carved their names and initials year after year. There were hearts with names in them. Callie wondered if she and David would ever carve their initials on this table.

"I'm hungry enough to eat two of everything. How about you?"

Callie longed for a bowl of chili, topped with cheese and sour cream, but she knew she couldn't do that to herself. It had been too hard, losing all that weight. "What's good here?" she asked brightly. *There, that's better.*

"I thought I'd go for a double taco with the works," he replied, smacking his lips.

"I don't think I could find a place to put all that. I'll just have fruit salad."

The waitress came and took their orders.

"Now that everything's over with, my nerves have settled down." David shuddered.

Callie was stunned. David had always gotten the lead. Did he really fear getting anything less?

"You were really nervous? But you're an old pro by now," she protested.

"I think that auditions and performances will give me the jitters for the rest of my life," he said, laughing. "The idea of offering myself up to a sea of critical eyes—it makes me crazy!"

"I know what you mean," Callie said. "When I had to read with you the other day, I was seriously considering death a viable alternative."

David chuckled. "You know something, Callie?" David reached across the table and took her hand. "You and I have a lot in common." His bright blue eyes met hers. "I'm really looking forward to finding out more," he said warmly.

Callie felt the color flood her cheeks. She smiled and looked down at the table. Could David Palmer really be saying these things to her? His words sang in her ears. Shyly she smiled at him. He squeezed her hand.

The waitress came with their food. David dug into his taco with incredible zeal. Callie could tell they had something else in common—they both loved food. David started to tell her about a Fred Astaire-Ginger Rogers movie, *Flying Down to Rio*.

"It was the first film they ever made to-gether," he explained. He described an incredible dance scene, and Callie got so caught up listening to him she almost forgot about losing the part of Sarah. Soon she and David were laughing, oblivious to the people around them.

"Hey, you two, mind if we join you?" came a voice from above.

Callie and David looked up to see Richie Sanders grinning down at them.

"My date's gone off to make a phone call, but she'll be back in a moment," he explained. He flashed a big smile, his glance lingering on Callie.

Richard was a senior and a member of the drama club. He had taken part in the musicals every year, but he played secondary roles. That left him plenty of time to be sports editor of the yearbook, to play basketball, and to get involved with just about every activity Kennedy had to offer. He was a real go-getter and very good-looking. Most of all, he was known for having a different girl on his arm every week.

Just when things were going so well, Callie said to herself. Her heart sank, and she stared down at the table. She didn't want David to see how disappointed she was, so she looked up quickly and smiled at Richard. But not before David had given her a strange look.

David stared at Callie for a brief second, then shook Richard's hand warmly. "I see you're going to be in the chorus again this year, Rich. Congratulations, buddy!"

"Thanks, Dave." Richard sat down next to Callie. "You were sensational at the auditions, Callie. Congratulations to you, too."

Callie tried to smile as brightly as she could, but she felt so awful being reminded that she had lost the part of Sarah, she just mumbled her thanks and stared down at the table again.

There was an awkward silence. Then Dave cleared his throat and said to Richard, "Hey, buddy. How come you got here so late? I thought you opened this place every afternoon."

"I had to stop by the yearbook office. I was looking over some contact sheets from last week's scrimmage."

"How do you think this year's team looks without Williams?"

"I don't know. Kennedy sustained a real loss when he graduated." Richard's attention wandered across the room; he was obviously searching for someone. His eyes flickered, and he waved. Callie looked in the same direction. No—it couldn't be!

Kim Crawford slid into the booth next to David.

"Have you two met Kim Crawford?" Richard asked, clearly waiting for their reaction to his prize date. "I'm sure you saw her at auditions. You have before you the next star of the Kennedy High musical!" he said dramatically.

Kim blushed when Richard said this, both pleased and embarrassed at his words. Callie choked at the echo of the same phrase David had used only days before.

Richard made introductions around the table. David smiled and shook Kim's hand warmly.

"Looks like you and I will be working together a lot," he said, grinning. "Ken Morgan is a perfectionist, so we'll probably get to know each other pretty well with all those rehearsals."

Callie was stung at the sound of the words she'd dreamed David would be saying to her. She had been trying so hard to have fun and forget about the show—the last person she wanted to see was Kim Crawford. Painfully she gazed across the table at the person who had walked away with her dream.

Kim was so pretty—tall, gracefully thin, with blond hair that swung almost to her waist. She had deep-set green eyes that spar-kled when she smiled, which she always seemed to be doing. She made Callie feel inadequate.

Kim and Richard ordered, and the conver-sation settled on auditions and the weeks of rehearsal that lay ahead.

"I'm so glad you're playing Adelaide, Callie," Kim said, smiling. "A local group performed *Guys and Dolls* in my old town, and the woman who played Adelaide stole the show. I think you and I will even get the chance to do a duet together."

"That'll be fun," Callie mumbled. It took everything she had to sound enthused. "You must be pleased to be playing Sarah," she said. *Couldn't Kim just dissolve or something?*

"I'm really thrilled," said Kim. "I never thought I would get the part." Her modest reply only made Callie more miserable. *This would be so much easier if Kim were a rotten person.*

"I have an idea," David said. "Let's look at our scripts and have a read-through! We can get an idea of the story line and everything."

Oh, no! Callie groaned to herself. Nothing could be more unbearable right then than having to watch David and Kim read their lines together.

"That sounds like fun," Richard agreed, taking his script out. "I'll play Nathan Detroit, for today. Come on, sweet Adelaide," he read, putting his arm on Callie's shoulder. "Sue me, sue me, what can you do me, I love you!" He laughed and gave her a hug.

Callie was feeling so miserable, she was beginning to wish she weren't there. She was unable to look anyone directly in the eye. *I'm just spoiling everyone's fun,* she thought to herself and reluctantly fished out her script. She couldn't look up at David as he started to read his lines to Kim.

Between mouthfuls of tacos, they all read the script, delivering their lines with enthusiasm. Everybody, that was, but Callie.

"C'mon, Cal—put some more life into it," David complained. "I know you can do better than that."

Instead of improving her delivery, Callie was even more discouraged by David's words. She desperately wanted to impress him, but she was so upset by Kim's presence and excellent reading that the harder she tried, the worse she sounded. The others were getting so into it that they almost stopped noticing Callie mechanically reading the words off the page. She couldn't look at David and Kim, who were so involved in their parts, and even though Richard tried to get her to respond to him, Callie plunged deeper and deeper into misery.

The afternoon was wearing on. David, Richard, and Kim seemed to be having a great time, laughing and joking and hamming it up. Finally Callie couldn't take any more.

"David, I promised my mother I'd help her with dinner," she blurted. "Do you think you could take me home now?" She hoped she sounded casual.

Everybody stopped to look at her. There was an uncomfortable silence.

"You didn't mention it before," David said awkwardly.

"I guess—I forgot, that's all."

"Well, sure. No problem."

Richard and Kim exchanged puzzled looks. Richard jumped up and said quickly, "It was really fun, Callie. I'm glad we ran into you guys this afternoon. We'll have to do this again."

Callie was afraid to meet David's eyes, and she was unwilling to look at Kim. She focused all her attention on Richard and said, "Absolutely, I'm looking forward to it," trying to sound enthusiastic.

David looked from Callie to Richard to Kim and shrugged his shoulders. Silently he led her to the car. As soon as they sat down, Callie heaved a sigh of relief.

David said nothing. He merely looked at Callie strangely and snapped the tape deck on. Music from *Guys and Dolls* flooded the Chevy. Quickly he shut it off.

They drove on in silence. Callie stared out the window, afraid to look him in the face. He'd been having a good time, and she'd made a scene. He tapped his fingers on the steering wheel and whistled. At one point he drove through a stop sign and then cursed himself for doing it.

I have to explain, Callie thought wretchedly. *I'd better swallow my pride and hope he'll understand. If I don't, he may never want to see me again.*

"David," Callie started tentatively. "I know you're upset about leaving so abruptly. Let me explain."

"I know precisely what was going on in there," he said curtly. "I really don't want to talk about it, OK?"

"David, please—" Callie pleaded.

"We're not babies anymore, Callie! Let's just forget the whole thing."

They pulled up to Callie's house in silence. Sighing, she let herself out of the car and turned to him.

"Thanks for the ride. I guess I'll see you tomorrow," she said tentatively.

"Right," he said flatly, eyes straight ahead.

Callie didn't dare look back as she crossed the lawn, but she knew from the roar of the engine that David was halfway down the block.

As she threw her books down on the kitchen table, her mother told her that Jennifer had called. "Oh, no," Callie said, then moaned. Nothing could make her feel worse than the thought of facing Jennifer.

Miserably she picked up the phone and dialed her friend's number.

"Callie? Is that you?" Jennifer said.

"Jen," said Callie, "I wanted to talk to you after trig, but you disappeared. I have to tell you how terrible I feel about getting the part of Adelaide after I talked you into wanting it so badly. Believe me, I know how it feels."

"Don't worry. I was upset at first, but I'm not anymore." Jennifer sighed. "It isn't *your* fault. It's probably just as well—I could never have learned all those lines, anyway."

Good old Jennifer.

"I guess you're really disappointed about losing out on Sarah," Jennifer said.

"You know how important that role was to me," Callie said sadly.

"Maybe we can send Kim Crawford back to where she came from," Jennifer said, trying to joke Callie into good spirits.

Callie forced a weak laugh.

"Well, you and David had a good time this afternoon at least, right?"

Callie's eyes were brimming with tears. "Wrong, Jennifer. Absolutely wrong."

Chapter Six

"You know," Jennifer said on the way to school the next morning, "maybe you're making this thing out to be worse than it really is."

"C'mon, Jen," was Callie's glum reply. "I told you everything that happened and the way he said, 'We're not babies anymore.' I'm sure he thinks I'm a spoiled brat who can't take it because I didn't get what I wanted."

"Maybe he just doesn't realize why the role of Sarah is so important to you. Did you tell him?"

"I didn't get a chance to say anything!" Callie cried. "I guess he just didn't want to hear 'a baby' complain."

"But what about Friday night?" Jennifer asked. "Dancing around the parking lot like a pair of lunatics! And the picnic on Sunday! He kissed you! Doesn't that mean anything?"

"I thought it did. I guess I was wrong." She laughed bitterly. "I'm driving him right into Kim's arms."

"But Kim was Richard's date!"

"That doesn't mean anything, Jen. I was *David's* date. When I think of all the time he and Kim will spend together in rehearsals, it makes me want to scream."

"I still think there's hope," Jennifer said. "If he asked you out in the first place, he must be interested in you, right?"

"*Was* interested, you mean," Callie replied.

"Callie, the guy's not a creep. He can't do an emotional about-face in two minutes. He was probably just angry, that's all. Give him a chance to cool off and then try to speak to him. He'll listen. I'm sure he will."

"Do you really think so, Jen?"

Jennifer took Callie by the shoulders and looked at her earnestly.

"Everybody's got a dream, Cal. Something that means more to them than anything else. This was yours. You worked so hard to lose weight, and you wanted that part so much. David will understand that. Maybe you didn't handle it as well as you could have, but you have good reason for feeling the way you did. Just talk to him."

"Maybe you're right," Callie said feebly. "I'll think about it."

The opportunity presented itself to Callie sooner than she expected. As she rounded the corner on the way to her locker, David whizzed by, practically knocking her over.

"I'm sorry," he muttered. "I guess I didn't see where I was—"

He stopped speaking as soon as he saw it was Callie. Callie was so nervous her knees were shaking, but she tried to cover up with a joke.

"That's OK. I always wanted to play football," she said, forcing a smile.

"Callie, I—" he said softly.

"David, I want to talk about yesterday." The words rushed from her lips. "Have you ever wanted something so badly—"

Suddenly David stiffened. He glared at her, his eyes like ice. "Like I said yesterday, let's drop it, OK? See you around."

Callie stood frozen, watching him stomp down the hall. Confusion flooded every part of her body. What had she done wrong? *Is a guy who refuses to listen really worth it?* Callie asked herself. But her heart was breaking. She'd lost the role, and now she was losing David. There wasn't anything left in her life to go wrong.

After school Callie went to Rosedale to change the date of the performance there. When she arrived, the receptionist told her that Mr. Stern had someone in his office and might be tied up for a while.

She sat down with the stack of magazines. She came across a survey in a fashion magazine titled "Are you a Fun Date?" With a mixture of interest and dread, she began to read.

She was so engrossed in the article that she didn't hear the squeak of metal wheels stopping directly in front of her.

"Young lady! Miss Lloyd," barked a voice.

Callie looked up to see Hattie Stevens.

"Mrs. Stevens! How are you?" Callie asked, startled.

"I'm living, that's about all. What are you doing here again?" the old woman asked.

"I'm seeing Mr. Stern about the performance we're going to do here. We have to change the date."

"Young people today can never make up their minds," Hattie muttered.

Callie smiled.

"So is this play going to be better than last

year's? Wouldn't be hard to do, if you ask me."

"Just for you," Callie said teasingly, "we're going to make it the best play Kennedy High ever staged."

"And I suppose you'll be in it, right? Singing and dancing in the chorus."

"Oh, no!" Callie protested. "I'm not in the chorus! I have one of the biggest parts. I'm playing the comedienne." Callie was shocked to hear herself defend the part of Adelaide.

"Young people are so full of themselves these days. So you get some great part, and you think you're running the world."

"It's not such a great part," Callie said softly.

"What's that you say? Speak up!"

"All I said was 'it's not such a great part,' " Callie replied halfheartedly.

"Some people are never satisfied. What's wrong with your part?"

"There's really nothing wrong with it, I guess," Callie said, confused. "It's just that I was hoping to get the lead, that's all."

"Well, tell me about the part you did get."

Callie repeated the description she'd read in the front of the script while Hattie listened attentively.

"I think that sounds like a terrific role!"

the old woman exclaimed. "Now what about the part you *didn't* get?"

The words "didn't get" swept through Callie like a cold wind. She sighed and reluctantly described the part of Sarah Brown.

"That Sarah sounds like a real sap, if you ask me," Hattie concluded. "All she gets to do is stand there and look pretty, sing a few songs. Any nitwit can do that. *You've* got a role that you can really do something with. You're the one who's going to make everybody laugh."

"But don't you see?" Callie protested. "I'm always the funny girl—and besides, I'm second best. Sarah is the lead, not Adelaide. I'm just not good enough to get the lead. I worked so hard this summer to lose weight so the director wouldn't think I was too fat. But *fat*," Callie said bitterly, "was not the problem. *I* was the problem. I'm just not good enough."

"If you want to feel sorry for yourself, that's your business. But you can also think about what a terrific chance you have to do a good job! If you don't want the part of Adelaide, why don't you just up and give it back?"

Callie was stunned by Hattie's sobering words. The silence spurred the old woman on. "And you know what else? With a part like this tootsie nightclub dancer, you can steal the show. You can leave sappy little Sarah in the dust!" In her enthusiasm Hattie almost jumped out of her wheelchair.

Callie couldn't help but laugh at her friend's unexpected vitality.

"So are you going to go out there and learn your lines and be a great actress and impress everybody?"

Suddenly Callie thought about David and the afternoon before. Her smile disappeared. "I guess so," she said without conviction. "Impress almost everybody, anyway."

"So who wouldn't be impressed?" Hattie was looking Callie straight in the eye.

Callie said nothing.

"OK, young lady. What's his name?"

Callie felt her face ablaze.

"Yahoo! Now we're getting somewhere. Tell me all about him."

"How do you know everything?" Callie asked, amazed.

"Let's just say I've been around the block a few times. Are you going to tell me about your young man or not?"

Callie hadn't shared her thoughts about David with anyone but Jennifer, and Jennifer was too optimistic to realize how awful the situation really was. Mrs. Stevens certainly wasn't going to run into anybody from Kennedy, so what harm could there be in telling her? Even though an old woman like Hattie probably couldn't understand, Callie figured it might help just to talk about it.

"Well, there's this guy in my school—" Callie started.

"Uh-huh."

"He's a senior, a year older than I am, and every year he gets the lead in the musical. He's very talented."

"This is all beginning to fall into place, if you ask me," Hattie said and giggled behind her hand.

"It's not what you're thinking!" Callie protested. "I really wanted the lead for *myself*. David had nothing to do with it!"

"Of course not," Hattie said simply.

"Really!" Callie said defiantly. She looked up to see a broad smile on the old woman's face.

"Well, maybe just a little bit," Callie said sheepishly. "He's really a nice guy, and I thought if we played opposite each other, we'd get to know each other better because we'd spend so much time rehearsing together, and—"

"Stop! Stop!" Hattie laughed. "So now your

young man will be playing with another young lady. Is she pretty?"

"*Very.* And really nice! I don't stand a chance against her!"

"Just because she's got the part you want doesn't mean she's going to get the boy you want. You're a perfectly lovely young lady, and I'm sure any young man would be proud to escort you."

Callie giggled at her friend's old-fashioned words.

"How well do you know this Romeo?" Hattie demanded.

"Last year we were in the musical together, but he had a girlfriend, who's gone now. We've had some great dates in the last week, but yesterday we went out after school, and I really blew it."

"Now why'd you do a thing like that?" Hattie had an exasperated look on her face.

"I certainly didn't *plan* on blowing it," Callie said defensively. "We went to one of the local school hangouts, and we were having a great time. Then *she* showed up, and I panicked. I couldn't handle it, and I behaved pretty badly for the rest of the afternoon. By the time he took me home, he was barely speaking to me."

"You blew it, all right," Hattie agreed. "But that doesn't mean you've lost him forever."

"You don't understand! David is one of the most popular guys at Kennedy. There isn't a girl there who isn't dying to go out with him. He's not going to waste his time on a jerk like me."

"I'm not so sure about that. I used to know a boy named Sam. I didn't treat him very well for a while—much worse than the one lousy afternoon you had. No matter how much Sam wooed me, I still flirted with all the other young gentlemen who came my way. I think you young people call it 'playing the field.' Sam ended up wasting a lot of time with this jerk—" Hattie pointed to herself. "He married her."

As Callie peered into the old woman's face, she noticed that Hattie had a faraway look in her eyes, and a smile was playing faintly on the corners of her mouth.

"Anyway, enough of that." Hattie snapped back. "Listen to your elders—all is not lost. Why don't you try to—"

"Miss Lloyd," the receptionist interrupted. "Mr. Stern is ready to see you."

Callie wished Mrs. Stevens had finished her sentence. What should she try to do?

"Mrs. Stevens?" she asked timidly. "Will you still be here when I'm through inside?"

"Naw—I have to go to the rec room before dinner. Can you imagine being *forced* to play bingo at my age?"

"Mrs. Stevens," the receptionist said in mock exasperation, "you know we don't force our residents to do anything they don't want to."

"Don't believe a word she says," Hattie said mischievously.

Callie concealed her laughter. "I really enjoyed talking to you, Mrs. Stevens. Is it OK if I come back and visit you again?"

"Not unless you call me Hattie."

"OK, Hattie." Callie grinned.

"And one more thing. When you come back, bring some Oreos—the food in this place stinks." She glared at the receptionist, who hid her smile behind a manila folder.

Callie laughed. "OK, you got it!"

Chapter Seven

Electricity was in the air when Callie walked into the auditorium. It was the first time the cast was officially together, and the kids who knew each other from previous plays were casually chatting, while the newcomers hung around, desperately trying to look a part of it. The only stranger who didn't seem to be having trouble was Kim Crawford.

Callie couldn't bear it. Kim was sitting near the front of the stage with David, Julia, Richard, and Ken Morgan around her.

Listlessly Callie dumped her books on a seat and looked around for Mike and Jennifer. She spied them walking through the back door and waved to them. They unloaded their books on top of hers.

"There's nothing I like better than a pop

quiz in math, right, Callie? Do you believe the nerve of that guy?"

"I thought I was looking at an extraterrestrial language," Callie agreed.

"Mike, Callie, Jennifer—come over here a minute!" called Ken. "I need to speak to you."

Callie panicked at the prospect of having to join David and Kim. She gave Jennifer a pleading look, but her friend just shrugged. The three of them made their way up to the stage.

"Richard, you can stick around if you want to," Ken said, "but what I've got to say is primarily for the rest of you. Julia is handing out a special rehearsal schedule. Because of the parts you're playing, you're all going to have to put in a lot of extra time."

"What does this have to do with me?" Jennifer asked, confused. "I'm just in the chorus."

Ken smiled. "You aren't *just* in the chorus, unless you want to be. I'd like you to be dance captain. That'll mean working with the entire cast to make sure they know left from right. You know what an impossible job that can be! You're the best person for it. How about it?"

Jennifer's face lit up. "I'd love to!" she cried eagerly. She turned to Mike, who squeezed her hand and grinned happily at her.

"OK. Back to work. Callie and Mike, you

two will have a lot of extra rehearsals together because of all the scenes you share. Same goes for you two," he said, looking at Kim and David.

Callie looked down at the floor.

"Callie and Kim have a few scenes together, as do David and Mike. It's all on the schedule. Basically what will happen is while Julia and Jennifer work onstage with the chorus, I'll be with the leads in the orchestra room. Jennifer, you'll be spending a lot of time with both groups, so I hope you weren't planning to get any homework done this term," he added with a laugh. "OK, Julia, get everybody ready for warm-ups. Guys, I need some help backstage."

Callie and Jennifer walked back to their seats. *It figures*, Callie thought painfully, *that I have extra rehearsals with everybody but David.*

Jennifer was on cloud nine. "Oh, Callie—I'm absolutely thrilled that Ken's asked me to be dance captain! I guess all those years of tap and ballet are finally paying off."

Callie was hardly paying any attention. "Did you see the expression on David's face when Ken mentioned all those extra rehearsals he and Kim would be having? He looked as if he doesn't mind a bit," she said sadly.

"What? Oh, come on, Callie, you're just imagining things. Don't bum out on me."

Mike came up behind them and wrapped his arms around Jennifer's waist, planting a kiss on her neck. "How 'bout it, Dance Captain?"

Jennifer turned and threw her arms around him.

Dejected, Callie started to walk away. She was feeling so low that she was even getting jealous of Mike and Jennifer.

"Hey, what's bugging her?" Callie heard Mike ask as she slinked away.

"Oh, let me talk to her. I'll tell you later," replied Jennifer.

Jennifer walked up to Callie and put her arm on her shoulder.

"Callie Lloyd, you have just got to stop feeling sorry for yourself. You'll never get David *that* way! Come on, pal. Cheer up. You know, you've got a great part. It wasn't the one you wanted, but it *is* a great part. You've got to pull yourself together if you want to be able to do it."

"Oh, Jennifer. I'm just so disappointed. First the part, and then David . . ." Callie had tears in her eyes. "But I guess everybody is right, I *am* acting like a baby. Let me just sit for a while. I'll try and cheer up."

"OK. But don't brood," said Jennifer. "I'll see you later."

Callie sat and thought for a long time. Everyone—Hattie, Jennifer—had said the same thing to her. She'd better try to get over this and make the best of what she had—or she might not have anything left!

When Julia screamed for warm-ups, Callie bounced out of her seat, threw her shoulders back, and joined the cast on stage.

As the weeks passed, Callie threw all her energy into learning her lines and perfecting her part. Even though the first performance was more than a month away, it was important for the leads to learn their lines, music, and blocking first so that the whole production could be pulled together.

Callie worked so hard and learned her part so well that she began to take pride in playing the part of Adelaide. Many people, especially Ken Morgan, complimented her on the way the role was taking shape. The one person who never said a word about her performance was David.

Since that afternoon at Moe's, he seemed to avoid Callie completely. One afternoon, as she was making her exit from the stage, she accidentally bumped into him as he ran on to do his scene. As they collided, he grabbed her shoulders and started to apologize. When he looked down and saw it was Callie, his face twisted into a strange frown, and he rushed onstage without another word.

Callie was in agony every time something like that happened. Why did he seem so angry, so disdainful of her? And why did he act like she didn't exist? Callie remembered that she once read somewhere that if a guy pretended you didn't exist, when you *knew* he knew you did, he was probably insecure. It was hard to convince herself that gorgeous David Palmer was insecure, but it made her feel a little better on occasion. But it was awful seeing David every day. As much as Callie tried to push him out of her mind, she always discovered that she was thinking about him again.

Callie wished she could discuss this more with Jennifer. But Jennifer was so tied up with her responsibilities as dance captain, that she and Mike were spending every spare moment together. She was seeing less and less of Jennifer—and to make matters even worse—David was getting very friendly with Mike. That make her feel even more left out.

The only person who paid the slightest attention to her was Howie Jensen, the rehearsal pianist. He always seemed to turn up wherever she was; he constantly asked her if she wanted extra practice on the piano, and in his nervous way, he was always telling her how terrific she was. Callie thought Howie was a very talented musician, but she just wasn't interested in him, and she was tired of his tagging along after her.

Maybe because she was lonely, or maybe because the only person she could talk to was Hattie, Callie found herself spending more and more time at Rosedale. The more she learned about the old woman, the better she liked her. It was more than sixty years since Hattie had been a teenager, but she seemed to understand Callie better than any of her friends. Callie loved to listen to her stories about "when *I* was a girl," and she got a kick out of watching Hattie wolf down the Oreos that they concealed from the nurses.

"When *I* was a girl," Hattie started one afternoon, "we didn't spend time on such foolishness as musicals. And girls never went to college. We learned how to cook and mend and make soap and butter, and by the time I was your age, I had been married almost a year. How do you like them apples?"

"But, Hattie," Callie said, "things are different now. If I were married at my age, I'd be practically the only one. Today women go to college and get good jobs. Some don't even *get* married."

"What a lot of balderdash. I say a woman isn't worth her salt who can't sew a button on properly," she replied, munching on a cookie. "I've heard all about this women's liberation stuff. Feh! I say men and women are here on this earth to live side by side and help each other. *That's* equality. Pass the cookies."

"I still want to go to college and have a career," Callie said resolutely. "I don't know exactly what I'll do—maybe I'll be an actress—but whatever I do, I can't imagine just staying home and taking care of a house and kids. My mom's got a great job with an ad agency, and I've always been well fed."

"I still don't like it," Hattie protested. "My daughters both call themselves career women. But do I ever hear from them? Ha!" she laughed bitterly. "Every couple of months one of them sends a check and says, 'Buy yourself something nice.' Can you beat that!" Hattie scowled.

Callie looked at her friend in amazement. In all the time they'd known each other, Hattie had never once mentioned anything about her daughters. She didn't even know Hattie had children. Callie's face expressed her surprise.

Hattie glared at her. "I don't want to talk about them. They live out on the West Coast. There. Don't ask me again." Hattie started to wring her hands in agitation. "If my Sam were still alive, *he* would never leave me in a place like this. Sam was so good to me."

"Why don't you live in California with your kids?" Callie ventured.

"Aw, they tried to get me to go out there, but I've lived in New York all my life, and I intend to die here," she said flatly. Hattie stared at the floor.

"Hey," Callie said cheerfully, "you want to play checkers? I'm sure I can get Nurse Dawson in the rec room to lend us a set—"

The old woman looked up. "Nah. How are we fixed for cookies?" she asked, peering into the box.

"If you eat another cookie, you'll turn into one," Callie said, offering her friend the box. "My mother always says that."

"How's that young man of yours? The one from the show? You haven't said a word about him in a long time."

"That's because there's nothing to tell,"

Callie snapped. "He acts as if I don't exist, and I try not to think about it too much."

"I can't say you sound like you're suffering over it," Hattie remarked. "I thought you were real sweet on this young man."

Hattie had a way of always dragging the truth out of Callie.

"To be honest, it breaks my heart," Callie said plaintively. "I think about him all the time. I just don't understand what I did that afternoon that was so awful. Why won't he even talk to me?"

"Have you done your best to be nice to him?"

Callie looked sheepishly at the floor.

"Not really. He seems so angry, I don't exactly put myself near him. But that's not what really upsets me."

"Pass the cookies."

"Remember that girl I told you about, the one who got the part I really wanted?"

"Tall, beautiful Kim," replied Hattie.

"Thanks a lot." Callie moaned. "When she first got to Kennedy, she dated a few different guys, each one only a couple of times."

"Did she date David?"

A pain shot through Callie. "No, but they may be going out now. Since rehearsals started, Kim hasn't been seen with one single guy, but she sure spends a lot of time with David."

"*That* doesn't mean anything," Hattie rejoined. "Just because they're together all the time, doesn't mean they're out necking every Saturday night."

"But why would she stop dating all these other guys?" Callie asked desperately. "I can't believe that nobody is interested in her. And David's hardly ever without a girlfriend. The only explanation I can think of is that they're perfectly happy with each other."

"That's the problem with young people these days," Hattie said, exasperated. "They're always jumping to conclusions. If I were you, young lady, I'd try to be just as nice as possible to your young man. It certainly can't hurt. And why don't you make friends with *Kim*? Maybe she'll spill the beans if you can get her to trust you."

"You're a sneak, you know that? Anyway, I tried that already, but she's not talking. I get the feeling she's trying to hide something. Whenever I ask her about her old high school or the town she used to live in, she changes the subject. I was about to give up on her."

"Nope. Give it another try. There's no better way of finding out what's going on between her and David than going straight to the source—that is, if she *is* the source."

"I guess you're right," Callie said solemnly. "And I suppose I'll find out—one way or the other."

"Hey, Hattie," called a voice from the door, "are you terrorizing that poor girl?"

"Who's that?" Callie asked, turning to face the door.

"That's nobody," Hattie muttered under her breath. The man in the doorway walked toward them slowly, leaning on a cane.

"Go on. Go away, Roy. We're talking girl talk in here. No codgers allowed."

"Is that any way to talk to your favorite beau?" he asked, laughing. "You'll give the young lady the impression I'm a mean old geezer."

"I'll buy that," Hattie snapped. "Can't you see that I've got company? Why don't you leave us alone!"

Roy's smile faded, and he fixed his eyes on the floor.

"Well, OK," he said dejectedly. "Just came by to see what you were up to, that's all. Beg your pardon, miss," he said, tilting his head.

"I'm Callie Lloyd," she said and smiled, trying to make up for Hattie's rudeness.

"Nice to meet you, Miss Lloyd. I'm Roy Aarons."

Hattie glared.

"I'll be on my way now," Roy said softly. "I didn't mean to interrupt."

Callie watched as Roy shuffled out of the room. When he was safely out of earshot, Callie gave Hattie an exasperated sigh.

"You weren't very nice."

"Aw, who needs him. He's always coming around here and bothering me—talking about the weather, asking to play checkers, telling me his stupid jokes."

"He's trying to be friendly! What's wrong with that? He seems like a nice man. You probably have a lot in common." Callie folded her arms.

"The only thing that Roy Aarons and I have in common is that we're *old*. I don't need to be reminded of that every second. Besides, I've got you."

For a moment Callie was silent, touched by her friend's affection. But she felt concerned, too. "I can't be here all the time. It would be good for you to get to know some of the people you live with," she said softly. "You've been here three years already, and the only person you see regularly is the doctor, for goodness sake. You don't want everybody to think you're a mean old *bat*, do you? Besides, you might even enjoy Roy's company if you gave him half a chance."

"What's so great about playing checkers and gin rummy all day?"

"You don't seem to mind it when you play with me," Callie said. "C'mon, give it a try. Do it for me."

Hattie chewed on her lip.

"Aw, OK. But on one condition."

"What's that?"

"He doesn't get any of our cookies."

"You're on." Callie smiled.

Chapter Eight

At the start of the next day's rehearsal, Callie noticed Julia Dougherty coyly sidling up to Kim, Jennifer, and a few of the other girls. The next minute she was beside Callie.

"I'm glad I caught you before rehearsal started, Cal," Julia whispered breathlessly.

"What's up? I noticed something was going on."

"Shhh! It's kind of a secret. I can't invite a lot of people, and I don't want anybody's feelings to get hurt."

Callie smiled to herself. The way Julia was dashing around and whispering was attracting plenty of attention.

"Invite a lot of people where?"

"I'm having a slumber party next weekend, Saturday night. Just some of the girls. Can you come?" She made it sound like the social event of the century.

Not unless Jennifer is going, Callie thought to herself. "Can I let you know? I have to check with my parents first."

"Yeah, sure," Julia replied, startled that Callie hadn't accepted immediately.

Callie caught up with Jennifer during a break. "What did you tell Julia about her slumber party?"

Jennifer's face broke out into a broad grin. "I was going to ask you the same thing! I told her I'd let her know. I don't think I could bear it if you weren't there."

Callie laughed. "What's the verdict, then?"

"Julia's not so bad," Jennifer reasoned. "She just tries too hard. Besides, it might be fun. Who else did she ask?"

"I saw her talking to Kim, Cathy, and Angela. I wonder if they'll go."

"Kim will. She and Julia have become really tight since rehearsals started. Or at least Julia has been hanging all over Kim."

"Well, let's go. We don't have anything to lose," Callie said. *And maybe a lot to learn,* she thought to herself.

Later that afternoon Howie Jensen called to Callie from the piano, after a run-through of one of her songs.

"I thought we ought to go over that number again," he said nervously. "I'm not sure you've got the rhythm right when you sing 'He bought me the fur thing five winters ago.'" Howie stared at the piano keys.

"OK, Howie. Maybe during break we can put in a few minutes on it."

"Take ten, everybody!" Julia screamed.

"I guess there's no time like the present," Howie said, smiling tentatively.

Callie leaned over the piano as Howie plunked out the notes one by one. Carefully she sang the rhythm back to him a few times.

"I think it's OK now, don't you?" she asked.

"It's—uh—just right." Howie fidgeted with the sheet music.

"Thanks a lot." Callie turned and saw David approaching them. In a panic, she started to flee.

"Wait!" Howie blurted out. "I was kind of wondering—that is, what are you—I mean, would you like to go to the Fall Festival dance with me this year?" His face went red as he stammered out the words.

The Fall Festival dance! She had forgotten all about it, between rehearsals and visiting Hattie—and here was Howie putting her on the spot while David was coming right at them. Callie's thoughts began to race. Howie was a nice guy, but not her vision of the ideal date.

"Howie, I-I can't," Callie stammered awkwardly. David was at the piano now, tapping his fingers, obviously waiting for *one* of them.

Howie's eyes returned to his faithful piano. "That's OK, Cal. I should have figured you'd have a date for the dance by now," he said dejectedly.

"Yes, sorry, Howie. I already have a date," she lied.

David stared at her.

"Thanks for your help with that passage," she said, trying to sound composed. "I'm sure I'll get it right next time."

"Yeah, sure."

"Callie!" A voice from the stage interrupted them. Richard Sanders motioned to her. "Can you come up here a sec?" he yelled. "Jennifer needs you to go over a dance routine."

"Sure, Rich," she shouted. David looked at her, and his startled expression gave way to one of ice.

Callie swallowed hard. "Were you looking for me, David?"

"No," he said quickly. "I have to ask Howie a question." His voice sent shivers down Callie's spine.

"Oh, OK," she replied, trying to sound

bright. "See you, then." As she walked toward the stage, she heard Howie say, "I think she's kind of nice." But strain as she might, she was too far away to hear David's reply.

Callie and Jennifer stood in the hall, waiting for Mrs. Harmon to put on her coat and drive them to the Doughertys' home across town.

"What did Howie say when you told him you already had a date?" Jennifer asked.

"He took it well enough, but you should have seen the expression on David's face, Jen. If looks could kill—"

"What did you expect, after he heard you say that?"

"What else could I say without hurting Howie's feelings? I didn't want to accept a date with anyone else just in case David and I work everything out. Boy, I've really screwed things up. David thinks I already have a date, so he'll never ask me now. On top of which he looked like he'd never speak to me again."

"Callie, there's something I think you ought to know. I didn't want to be the one to have to tell you this, but . . ."

Callie tensed.

"I heard from Julia that David asked Kim

to the Fall Festival dance yesterday," Jennifer said quietly.

Tears welled up in Callie's eyes. "I guess I'm not surprised," she said. "They spend so much time together. It was inevitable that they'd fall for each other sooner or later."

Jennifer put her hand on Callie's shoulder. "Look, I know it seems like the end of the world," she said sympathetically, "but you'll get over—"

"I wish I had a dollar for every time those words were spoken!" Callie snapped. "Oh, I'm sorry, Jen. Never mind. Let's not talk about it, OK?"

"Right."

The trip to Julia's house seemed endless, and Mrs. Harmon chattered nonstop about the slumber parties she had gone to when she was a girl. Callie sat glumly in the back seat.

They finally pulled up at Julia's. After saying goodbye to Mrs. Harmon, Jennifer looked at Callie and said, "You didn't say *one* word in the car. You can't act like that tonight, or people are going to ask a lot of embarrassing questions. The truth comes out at parties, you know. Get yourself together."

Callie smiled weakly as Jennifer rang the bell. "I'll try my best."

Mrs. Dougherty took their coats as Julia escorted them into the kitchen. Kim was busy putting together a salad while Angela and Cathy set the table.

Callie swallowed hard. "What can we do?" she asked, trying to sound cheerful. Jennifer gave her a wink.

"I guess everything's just about done," Julia said, checking the table. "Why don't you get some glasses out of the cabinet, Jen. Callie, you can get the ice cubes from the freezer."

Julia opened the oven door to check on the pizzas, which were being kept warm.

"Mmmmm—I just *love* pizza!" Cathy exclaimed.

"We always aim to please." Julia laughed. "Why doesn't everyone sit down?"

The girls took their seats as Kim placed a large bowl of lettuce and tomatoes on the table. "This is to make up for all the guilt we're going to have about the pizza," she said, giggling.

Callie smiled. She really did like Kim. If only her jealousy wouldn't get in the way.

"OK, everybody, dig in!" cried Julia, setting one of the pizzas in the center of the table.

As they ate, they talked and laughed about school, clothes, and the musical.

"Isn't it great to be able to spend time together *without* being stuck at rehearsal?" remarked Angela, helping herself to a third slice of pizza.

"I'll say," agreed Kim. "I love working on the show, and I'm having lots of fun, but it's so time-consuming! Ken really works us hard. It's nice to have time to do other things, like this."

"You mean you'd rather be here than running lines with David Palmer?" Julia asked teasingly.

Callie kicked Jennifer under the table.

"Kim," Jennifer said quickly, "tell us about the town where you used to live in Ohio. Did your school put on musicals?"

"Yes, but it wasn't the big deal that it is here. Nobody cared much."

"Wow!" Julia exclaimed. "I can't imagine a school where drama isn't a top priority!"

"That's one reason I really like Kennedy. I'm hoping to make a career out of the theater."

"Gee, I don't have any idea what I'll do when I grow up," Cathy said.

Everyone laughed.

"I don't, either," admitted Angela. "But I really like biology. Maybe I'll be a doctor."

"Ugh!" Julia groaned. "All that blood and guts."

"Angela, if you're going to become a doctor, hurry up. I think I need my stomach pumped." Jennifer groaned.

"I'm full, too," Kim said.

"Why don't we clean up and then go up to my room and listen to records?" Julia suggested.

After the last dish was dried and put away, the girls bounced upstairs and switched on the stereo. They sat, talking and laughing for a while. Then Julia said, "Hey—I have a great idea. Let's tell each other's fortunes!"

"How do we do that?" Angela asked.

"I left my crystal ball at home," Callie said.

"All we need is a deck of cards and some imagination." Julia rummaged through her desk until she found the cards. "It's easy. I'll do Kim's fortune first. Watch."

Kim squirmed. "I feel like a guinea pig. Do someone else."

"Don't worry. I'm not going to predict an untimely death or anything like that. This game tells your fortune in love!"

Julia busied herself arranging the four kings in a row on the floor as the others looked on with interest.

"OK, Kim, pick a card, and without looking at it, put it aside for later." Kim did as she was told.

"All you have to do is ask questions, and the cards will answer them for you. But first you must name the four kings after different guys you know. Preferably boys who have *particularly* caught your eye," Julia said coyly.

"But I hardly know anybody at Kennedy—I just got here!" Kim protested.

"We'll help you," Cathy said, excited.

"It's more fun when we know all the guys anyway," Julia advised.

"Do I have to be in love with them?"

"Only the cards will tell." Julia started to giggle. "Why don't we start with your date for the Fall Festival dance, lucky David Palmer?"

Callie and Jennifer exchanged looks.

"He'll be the king of hearts," said Julia.

"I know Richard Sanders," Kim ventured. "The king of clubs."

"Now you're getting the idea," praised Julia.

"I really don't know anybody else. Why don't you tell somebody else's fortune?"

"No," Julia said with a wave of her hand. "If we can't think of anybody interesting, we can put in somebody funny."

"How about that nerd, Howie Jensen—the one who plays the piano?" suggested Angela. Her choice evoked a round of laughter.

"Hold it!" Callie cut in. The guilt she felt

over refusing to go with him to the dance suddenly inspired her to defend him.

"What's the matter?" Cathy asked.

Callie saw that all eyes were glued on her, waiting to hear what she had to say. At the last minute she chickened out.

"N-nothing," she stammered. "I just thought it might be fun to name one of the kings after a teacher. Like old man Weaver or somebody." *Coward.*

"Callie, what a great idea!" screamed Jennifer. "Could you imagine 'happily ever after' with that old bat?" Jennifer faked a swoon.

"OK, attention, everybody," said Julia, ever the stage manager. "So we have Richard, David, Howie, and Mr. Weaver. Now, all you have to do is ask a question that can be answered by a name. When the suit of the card I turn over matches the suit of the king it lands on, we have the answer. Go on, ask a question."

"Let's see . . . OK. Who's the cutest of them all?"

Slowly Julia turned over the cards. She tried to be as dramatic as possible, looking every girl in the eye as she went through the deck, putting cards on the kings. Finally, a card matched the suit of a king; it was in the clubs family.

"Richard!" everybody cried at once.

"Richard's pretty cute," said Kim.

"I think David's a lot cuter," Julia said. Callie shot Jennifer another look.

"I don't know what else to ask," Kim said helplessly.

"I know!" Jennifer cried. "Who's going to make the most money?"

Julia turned over the cards.

"Howie!" they shrieked.

"That's probably true," said Callie. "He's pretty talented."

"But, Callie, he's such a nerd," Cathy said and groaned.

"Who loves me the most?" asked Kim.

"Ooo—that's a good one," Angela said.

The girls waited breathlessly for the cards to match.

"David!" said Julia, a knowing look in her eyes.

Kim blushed. It did not go unnoticed by Callie.

"Who's going to leave Kim for another woman?" Jennifer asked.

"That's a nasty one!" Julia said with glee. She turned over the cards. "David again!"

Maybe there's something to this card game, thought Callie sarcastically.

"Who's going to be on the cover of *Time* magazine?" asked Angela.

"You don't need cards to know the answer to this one," Jennifer said. "One day old man Weaver is going to blow up the entire school with one of his chemistry experiments, and it's going to be *big* news."

Julia dealt the rest of the cards without reaching a match.

"Oh, my God—I've got to know!" cried Angela. "Now what do we do?"

Julia was obviously enjoying her role as fortune teller. "Ah, my eager subjects—we will never know."

Protests rang out from the circle, and pillow after pillow swooped down upon Julia.

"But what about that other card? The one Kim put aside at the beginning," asked Callie.

"I thought you'd never ask." Julia reached for the card with a flourish. She looked at each girl and solemnly recited, "This card reveals the name of the man Kim Crawford will marry. The six of us alone will share the secret."

"And the winner is—"

"Shut up, Jennifer, this is exciting!"

Slowly Julia turned over the card and moved to place it atop the proper king. Old man Weaver.

The laughter was deafening.

"Can I be a bridesmaid?" asked Callie, choking.

"I'm sure you two will be very happy together." Angela gasped.

"You, dummy—he's already married!"

"Scandal and intrigue—I love it!" Julia giggled. She put on the straightest face she could and in her most mysterious voice uttered, "Believe me, zee cahds nevah lie."

When the laughter finally died down, Jennifer spoke up.

"You're not going to believe this," she said, "but I'm hungry again."

Late that night Callie awoke, tossing in her sleeping bag. Gradually she realized that she was not in her own room but on the floor at Julia Dougherty's house, surrounded by the sleeping bodies of her friends. A strange noise had awakened her. She listened carefully for a minute. Then she heard it again. Someone was crying.

She became aware of a figure huddled by the window. Careful not to trip over the arms and legs sprawled in every direction, Callie tiptoed over. It was Kim.

"What's the matter?" she whispered. "My snoring can't be that bad."

Kim looked up. Her face was stained with tears, and her wet cheeks shone in the glow of a street lamp.

"It's nothing, Callie. Just go back to bed."

"But you're crying. Here, let's go in the den where we can talk and not disturb anybody." On the way out of the room, she grabbed a box of tissues.

As Callie silently led Kim to the den, her mind raced with curiosity about the source of Kim's tears. Could it have something to do with David?

"Let's sit over here," Callie said gently, turning on a light in the den, and pointing toward a couch. "Did you have a fight with your parents? Are you nervous about the play? Is it a guy? I know, Julia's driving you up the wall."

"No," Kim said, laughing weakly. Kim grabbed a tissue and blew her nose, and the girls sat in silence for a few minutes. Finally Kim sighed and began.

"Callie, I haven't told anybody at Kennedy about this because—well, you'll understand when you hear the whole story. Do you promise to keep my secret?"

Callie touched her lightly on the shoulder.

"Back in Ohio, I have a boyfriend, Greg. We've been going out for two years—ever since

113

we met. He's really wonderful. His family lives on a farm." Kim's tears suddenly returned.

"It's OK, Kim. It's good to let it out," Callie said in a soothing voice.

"I think I'm going to have to buy the Doughertys a new box of tissues to make up for these." She sniffled and blew her nose.

"Greg and I are—were—*are* very serious about each other. We've even talked about getting engaged after college."

Boy, am I glad to hear that! Callie said to herself. "So what's the problem?" Callie asked.

"My parents. They like Greg and everything, but ever since we moved to New York, they've been lecturing me about dating other people. They think I'm too young to know what I want. I know we moved because of my father's transfer, but I think they were just as happy to get me away from Greg. My mother always complained that we spent too much time together, that I didn't make an effort to get to know anybody else, and that I was locking myself into something. Maybe that's true, but I *love* Greg." Kim's tears sprang fresh.

So she's not in love with David.

"I don't want anybody here to know because if they think I'm taken, nobody would ever ask me out. My mother would never understand that."

"I understand," Callie said sympathetically.

"But that's not why I'm upset tonight," Kim resumed, wiping her eyes. "Today I got two letters—one from Greg and one from Jane, my best friend. Greg wrote to tell me that he won't be able to fly out for the show, something I'd really been counting on."

"He must have had a good explanation," Callie offered hopefully.

"He said he didn't have the money or something. But that's not the worst part. Jane's letter told me that—that Greg is taking another girl to the annual harvest dance at the high school—"

Callie put her hand on Kim's shoulder. Slowly it dawned on Callie. This was her chance!

"Maybe he just doesn't want to feel left out. Would you want him to sit around and mope while his friends are out having a good time? Maybe he's just taking her as a friend—just," Callie ventured carefully, "as David is taking you to the Fall Festival dance here at Kennedy."

Callie held her breath as she waited for Kim to answer. Kim blew her nose again, but she didn't say a word.

Chapter Nine

During the next week, rehearsals continued practically nonstop. Kim and David were together constantly.

The weekend seemed endless to Callie. The Fall Festival dance was that Saturday night, and on Sunday Jennifer called and said that Kim and David had looked pretty cozy at the dance. What about Greg? Callie wondered. Had Kim decided to give up on him and concentrate on David instead?

When Callie walked into rehearsal on Monday, she was feeling very depressed. Even with her own problems, however, she was instantly aware that something was wrong, something to do with the show. Instead of the prerehearsal chatter, she was greeted by a roomful of hushed whispers. Ken called her to the stage, where he was talking to David, Mike, Jennifer, and Julia.

"Mrs. Crawford called me this morning. Kim has strep throat with complications," he said soberly, "and will be out indefinitely."

Jennifer and Callie looked at each other, stunned.

"It will be up to the six of us to make sure the show doesn't fall apart. For the time being, we have to assume that Kim will not be well in time to go on. Jennifer, get hold of a script and start learning Adelaide's part, and Mike, you work with her. This means that you," he said, looking at Callie, "will take over for Kim. Start learning your lines right away. Julia, it will be up to you to work with Callie and Jennifer and teach them their blocking and stage business. David, you and Callie will spend every spare moment working together on your scenes. Lunch periods, study halls—everything."

They received the news in silence. Callie's heart pounded. She felt panicky. With the nursing home performance on Thursday night and less than two weeks until the real performances at Kennedy, how could they manage without Kim?

Ken continued, "Fortunately, Rosedale won't be too tough because we'll just be doing a few songs in costume, with a little bit of dancing. But no dialogue or sets. You know each other's songs by now anyway."

Ken smoothed his hair back with his hands, something he did only when agitated. "We'll work the rest of this out later. Callie and Jennifer should start reading for the new parts today."

Dazed, Callie and Jennifer went back to their seats. For a long while, neither one spoke. Suddenly Jennifer burst into laughter. Callie looked at her in astonishment.

"Callie, don't you see? You're playing Sarah, I'm playing Adelaide—it's just as we planned before auditions!" Jennifer started to laugh again.

Callie felt uncomfortable. Although Jennifer had said that she didn't mind losing the part of Adelaide, Callie had always thought that Jennifer was only trying to make her feel better. Now that she seemed so excited at getting a chance at the part, Callie felt even guiltier.

"I guess we both have a lot of late nights ahead of us," Jennifer said, not minding a bit. "*You* must be really thrilled. You're finally getting the chance you longed for!"

"I guess so," Callie said, but to her surprise, she wasn't thrilled at all. She had worked very hard on Adelaide and by now took great pride in the job she'd done. It's true that she'd dreamed all summer of playing the romantic lead, but to lose Adelaide now was like losing a part of herself.

And there was David. Fate was giving her the opportunity to spend time with him, maybe even patch things up, but she was frightened. Ever since that day at Moe's, he'd been angry at her and seemed to avoid her at all costs. She had tried to get over him, but it still hurt. Could she bring herself to face him now?

I have no choice, she brooded. *Like it or not, David Palmer, we're stuck with each other.*

They rehearsed that night, during lunch the next day, after school, and Tuesday night. Ken carefully selected the songs to be performed at Rosedale so it wouldn't be too hard for Jennifer and Callie to learn them, but there was still a lot of work to do.

Much to Callie's relief, she didn't have to face David as much as she'd feared. All their rehearsals included other people, so they were never alone together. He was very businesslike in his treatment of her, doing what was required of him onstage, without any of the usual kidding around that accompanied rehearsals. Callie secretly longed for a sign of acceptance from him, but none came. Perhaps it was all for the best that they concentrated on their roles instead of their relationship, Callie rationalized.

It was easy for Callie to pick up Sarah's songs for the nursing home performance, but she spent every spare minute away from rehearsals trying to learn Sarah's lines. She had no time for homework or household chores, and she knew she wouldn't be able to visit Hattie that week. Until then, she had managed to visit the old woman twice a week. Callie missed her—but worse than that, she felt terrible knowing that no one else visited her. Callie hoped that Hattie would decide to give Roy Aarons half a chance, but she doubted it.

On Wednesday afternoon, rehearsal was devoted entirely to the songs they would perform at the nursing home. Callie and David were on stage delivering a duet while Ken watched them from the house. Suddenly they were interrupted by a cry from Julia.

"Cut, you guys!" she bellowed.

Ken approached the stage, script in hand. "OK, listen. I realize you've had to take over this part on short notice, Callie, but I know you can do better than this."

Her eyes fell to the floor.

"Talent is talent, Cal, and you were doing such a superb job as Adelaide. I know you're just not giving it your all," Ken continued gently.

Suddenly his tone changed.

"As for you, David, you've been rehearsing this role for weeks, so I don't know what *your* excuse is." Ken's voice displayed annoyance. "I realize it's difficult to change partners halfway through production, but you'll just have to try harder."

"What exactly am I doing wrong?" he asked sheepishly.

"It's not that you're doing anything *wrong.* But the whole scene lacks life. You look like a pair of wooden soldiers up there. Complete strangers. Loosen up. Act like you're enjoying it. There seemed to be more chemistry between you two at auditions."

Miserable, Callie watched Ken walk down the stairs and take his seat in the house. His words about chemistry between David and her stung sharply. She and David couldn't get it together offstage—or onstage! David was such a good actor, he must really hate her to let it affect his performance like this.

They ran the scene again, and Callie doubled her efforts. She tried as hard as she could to enjoy what she was doing. Maybe if she pretended David was a guy she was madly in love with, it would be easier. But she *was* in love with him—something she had tried to suppress since that awful afternoon at Moe's. The problem was, she was in love with a guy who couldn't stand the sight of her—

"Cut!" screamed Julia.

Ken was back on the stage. "It looks like we're not going to accomplish anything today. I have to get to Mike and Jennifer, but you aren't off the hook. Get into the orchestra room and work on this together." Ken looked at them with pleading eyes. "Please—I want the performance at Rosedale tomorrow night to go well."

Callie and David exchanged embarrassed looks, the first real communication they'd shared since their last date. Silently they trudged to the orchestra room.

David flipped on the lights and heaved a sigh. "We may as well get started. Which scene would you like to work on?"

"How about the one we were just doing?" Callie suggested nervously.

"I still have a bad taste in my mouth from

that one. Why don't we try the duet in Act Two?" he asked flatly.

"Don't we need Howie?"

"I can play enough to give us our starting notes, and we can take it from there."

Act Two. That's the one where he puts his arms around Sarah. He won't be able to throw any feeling into this one.

"Ready?"

"Sure," she said, hoping she sounded convincing.

David went over to the piano, plunked out the notes and started to sing. After a verse, he gave Callie her opening note, and she joined him. Soon his arms were wrapped around her waist as they moved to the music. It was a mechanical gesture at best, and Callie felt every muscle in her body tense. Suddenly David dropped his arms.

"This isn't working," he said flatly.

"Maybe we just need to practice some more—"

"That's not it, and you know it," he said, pacing the room.

"There was a time when we didn't have this kind of trouble," Callie said softly. "And you didn't seem to be having a problem with Kim. Why don't you just pretend I'm Kim? That would solve all our problems."

"And who will you pretend *I* am, Richard Sanders?" he shot back.

Callie's mouth fell open in disbelief. Suddenly David looked away.

"Richard Sanders? What on earth does he have to do with this?"

"Oh, come on, Callie. What do you take me for?" he snapped.

"David, I have no idea what you're talking about—"

"Great acting, Callie, but if that's the way you want to play it, I'll refresh your memory. I thought you'd practically jump into his arms the day he walked in on us at Moe's. And when you told Howie Jensen that you had a date for the Fall Festival dance and neither of you showed up, I didn't need further proof. Explain *that* one!"

"David, listen. I don't know how you came up with this, but it simply isn't true."

At that moment the door was flung open, and Julia stuck her head in.

"OK you guys. Ken wants you on stage now. I hope you've worked everything out."

David spun on his heels and was out the door.

"Why don't you just ask Richard!" Callie shouted after him.

But he was around the corner by then.

125

Callie walked into the house, flung her books on the sofa, and dialed Jennifer's number.

"I'll get her, dear," said Mrs. Harmon. "That is, if I can tear her away from that script."

Callie fidgeted as she waited for Jennifer to come to the phone.

"What's up, Cal? Aren't you busy learning your lines?" came the voice through the receiver.

Forlornly Callie poured out every detail of her conversation with David that afternoon.

"Richard Sanders? Where did he get that idea?" Jennifer asked in amazement.

"Who knows."

"Callie, this is great!" Jennifer said joyously.

"You're kidding, right?"

"Don't you see? He's *jealous*. He's angry because he *cares* about you. You two have a communication problem, that's all. Once you get a chance to explain everything, it'll all work out. If you were walking around thinking what he's been thinking, wouldn't you be hurt, too?"

"But what about Kim, Jennifer? You know as well as I do that they've been spending a lot of time together. Even if David did care for me once, isn't it possible he's started dating Kim since then?" Callie didn't mention that Kim had a boyfriend in Ohio. If David didn't know, what would stop him from falling for Kim, anyway?

"I don't know, Cal," Jennifer said thoughtfully. "They *have* spent a lot of time together, and I know he's been to visit her since she got sick."

Callie sighed.

"But that doesn't mean there's anything going on!" Jennifer protested. "Look. Get a good night's sleep. You have a performance to do tomorrow evening. And the first chance you get, talk to David and explain everything."

"But he won't listen to me! He just charges off the minute I open my mouth," Callie wailed. "It's just hopeless."

"No, it's not, Cal," Jennifer said, comforting her. "We'll think of some way to make him listen."

Sure, Callie thought to herself.

"Cal, get a good night's sleep. We'll work on it tomorrow."

"OK, Jen. Maybe you're right. And Jen"— Callie paused—"thanks a lot."

At Rosedale the next evening, there was such a frenzy of makeup, costume adjustments, and last-minute rehearsals that Callie didn't even have a chance to talk to Jennifer. At one point Callie noticed David and Mike in a very animated conversation. David was hitting his head with his hand—as if he were trying to knock his lines into his brain. *Last minute jitters*, thought Callie to herself.

Callie sneaked a look at the audience from behind the curtain. Her eyes searched the small auditorium for Hattie. She spotted her in the second row. True to form, she had a scowl on her face.

Suddenly Julia rushed in, whispering, "Places, everybody!" A hush fell over the cast as they arranged themselves backstage. Callie didn't have to go on right away and waited quietly in the wings.

The curtain went up to a burst of applause. Mike Selak, Richard Sanders, and Chuck Phillips started to deliver their trio with zeal. Callie felt a tug at her elbow. She turned to see Jennifer squeeze in beside her.

"Look at Mike—isn't he doing a great job?" Callie said.

Jennifer beamed. "I only date talented men. Did you talk to David yet?"

"No," Callie said. "I didn't—"

"Shush!" Julia whispered angrily.

Both girls glared at her—but shut up. Jennifer was on next, so she took her place in the wings.

After Jennifer's song, Callie and David walked onstage. The minute David started singing, Callie noticed a complete turnaround in his performance. Somehow, he had regained all the enthusiasm and liveliness he had exuded when rehearsing the part with Kim. Callie was stunned, but she responded to him immediately, and together they brought the house down. When they entered again for their love song, they were greeted by a loud round of applause.

David winked at Callie and started to sing. This time when he took her in his arms, she felt as if he really meant it. Callie felt a warm rush flood her body as he leaned over to kiss her at the end of the song.

When the entire cast joined them on stage for the finale, Callie could see Hattie beaming up at her from the audience. Callie felt guilty about ignoring her friend. She wanted to see her and explain everything.

But the big thing on her mind was David! Her head was just swimming. His performance was so different from the day before. While they were onstage, their arms around each other, it felt so natural, as if their problems of the last few weeks had never existed—as if he loved her!

"He really *is* a good actor!" she said to herself sarcastically. But deep down inside she knew it wasn't just acting. Something *was* different.

While she was changing in the dressing room, Callie felt so torn. She had to see David, but she couldn't walk out without saying hello to Hattie.

"Callie Lloyd! You come out here this minute!" she heard a familiar voice bark. Her conflict was resolved for her. Outside the dressing room, Hattie Stevens was sitting in her wheelchair, a big grin on her face. Callie gave her a warm hug and started to apologize for not having come to see her.

"Oh, hush up, young lady! A big star like you has more important things to do than visit an old bat like me," Hattie said, cackling.

Just then Jennifer walked out, and Callie called her over.

"It's about time my two best friends met," Callie announced, beaming. "Hattie, this is Jennifer Harmon."

"Hi," Jennifer said shyly.

"How ya' doin, kid?" Hattie replied robustly. "You did a great job up there, but frankly I'm a little confused. I thought *you* were going to play Adelaide," she said, poking Callie in the ribs.

"I was!" Callie laughed. "It's a long story. I'll tell you—"

Suddenly David Palmer whizzed around the corner. He stopped dead in his tracks when he saw Callie and Jennifer talking to Hattie. For a brief instant his eyes met Callie's, then he turned and walked away.

"Callie, I have to tell—"

Jennifer was interrupted by Hattie blurting out, "Now what was that all about!"

"I don't know," said Callie. "Come on, I'll fill you in on everything that's happened as I take you back to your room. Jen, go on without me. Mike's waiting for you. I'll call my brother to pick me up later."

"OK. Just tell me the second you see me tomorrow," said Jennifer, rushing off to look for Mike.

"Now, I want to hear every detail!" demanded Hattie as she and Callie went down the corridor. "What in thunder is going on?"

Chapter Ten

The next morning Callie slept through her alarm. It was almost eleven when the sound of the phone woke her up. She jumped out of bed and ran to answer it.

"I guess I woke you," came her mother's voice through the receiver.

"Mom! I must have overslept. Don't worry, I'll get dressed right away and ride my bike over to school and—"

"Callie, calm down, honey. Don't worry about school," her mother said reassuringly. "I took one look at you when you walked in last night and knew you'd never make it out of bed this morning. I let you sleep on purpose. Take the day off—you're running yourself ragged."

"Mom, you're great. Having a good day at work?"

"Better than usual, actually—the agency just landed a big ice-cream account, and Mr. Farlowe is putting me in charge."

"That's great, Mom. Do we get free samples?"

"Never mind that. I assume you'll be going to rehearsal this afternoon?"

"The plague couldn't keep me away," Callie said emphatically. "The closer we get to performance, the more practice I need."

"OK. See you later. If we're not home when you get in, it's because I made your father take me out to dinner to celebrate the new account."

Callie hung up the phone and went in to shower. As the water ran over her, she thought about the night before at the nursing home. *What had gotten into David?* she mused *Maybe I'm just imagining things. After all that's happened, last night can't possibly mean a thing. We seem to have had so many misunderstandings.*

Then she remembered that Jennifer had said she wanted to talk to her the minute she got to school. Callie jumped out of the shower. "I've got to hurry!"

"Where have you been all day?" Jennifer screamed as Callie walked into the auditorium. "I was afraid you'd jumped ship. If this production lost you *and* Kim, we'd really have a disaster on our hands."

"I'm fine, don't worry. Just overslept! Did make my history class, though." Callie grinned.

"You'd better go tell Ken before he gets hysterical."

Callie saw him talking to Howie by the piano. She dumped her script on a seat and called to him as she approached.

"Callie Lloyd, am I glad to see you!" Ken exclaimed. "When you didn't show up for class this morning, I thought we were done for."

"Don't worry, Chief. I'm fit as a fiddle." Callie laughed, giving him a salute.

"If I weren't so happy to see you, I'd give you you-know-what for cutting my class. Go get your script. We still don't know if Kim is coming back. You've got a lot more polishing to do. And, Callie—"

"Ken?"

"After last night I have no doubt about your ability to carry off this role. I don't know what happened to you and David, but whatever it is, it's working."

Callie ran up the aisle to her seat, where she noticed something sitting on top of her script. As she got closer, she saw a single white rose. Puzzled, she leaned over and

135

picked it up. There was a small card attached. She tore open the envelope.

"Callie," she read. "Let's talk during the break. David."

She looked up to see David sitting in the shadows several rows behind. His gaze was earnest and his smile tentative.

Confusion flooded Callie's thoughts. Her eyes returned to the small white card. Did this, *could* this mean that he wanted them to get back together? Or was he just trying to be friends?

She felt his eyes on her, even at that distance. She looked up and smiled back at him, and David leaped from his seat and was at her side.

"Callie," he said softly, "I've been such a jerk about everything. I've got so much to say to you."

Her eyes met his. "I've got a lot to tell you, too. But I just don't know where to start," she said quietly.

"Callie," Julie called from the stage, "it's time to rehearse the mission scene."

"Coming," she called back. "David, I —"

"Go. They need you on stage," he said, squeezing her hand. "I'll be here."

Callie flew to the stage, carried by the joy of knowing that somehow, everything between

David and her was going to be all right. She burned to know what he'd wanted to say when Julia called, but more than anything, she was filled with a sense of relief. If David hadn't had time to speak then, his eyes said everything Callie longed to hear.

Callie and David were huddled together on the radiator in the hallway, away from the rest of the crowd.

"If Mike hadn't set me straight before the performance last night, I'd still be thinking you were in love with Richard Sanders. When he walked into Moe's that day and you freaked out," David said, "all I could think was that you were interested in *him* and went nuts because you were stuck between the two of us. I was going to swallow my macho pride and say something the day you were talking to Howie at the piano, but then you said you had a date for the dance. I was sure it was Richard. When neither of you showed up, I figured he'd planned some incredible night out for the two of you. That's just his style. Boy, was I jealous! Thank goodness for friends like Mike."

"Oh, David! Part of it was my fault. I acted like such a jerk at Moe's. I can see how easy it was for you to read all that into the situation!

But I thought *I* would die when Kim walked in. I was so jealous I could hardly look you in the face. Richard and the table were the only things I could concentrate on without falling apart. I should have told you how much the part of Sarah meant to me. I know you would have understood. But when you said Adelaide was such a good part, I was afraid you would think I was a spoiled brat, just acting like a baby."

David gently pushed her hair away from her eyes. "Are you still sorry you were cast as Adelaide?"

Callie thought a moment. "No, no, I'm not. I've kind of grown attached to that dumb bombshell." Callie laughed softly.

"You know what? So have I."

He cupped her face in his hands, and their eyes were riveted together. Slowly he leaned over and kissed her. Callie circled her arms around his shoulders.

"I'm so glad to have you back," he whispered hoarsely. "I was a fool not to listen in the first place. I'll never do that again. I can't tell you how I've missed you."

Callie felt a flush of warmth spread over every limb as David hugged her hard.

"What do you say about going for a ride in

the country and a fall picnic Sunday, Ginger?" he asked, stroking her hair.

"But I've got so much to do," Callie protested. "Not only do I have to learn Sarah's lines, but I've got to keep up with Adelaide in case Kim gets better."

"I hope she does. You were born for the role of Adelaide, and I want to see you bring the house down."

Callie smiled warmly. "When the roles were first cast, I felt like life was over," she said thoughtfully. "I didn't want to be typecast as the comedienne. I wanted to prove to myself that I could play the leading lady instead of having everybody laugh at me. But I have so much more *fun* playing Adelaide. If Kim doesn't get better and I have to go on as Sarah, I'll feel as if a part of myself is missing."

"Here's to Kim's speedy recovery." David smiled and toasted with an imaginary glass. "Now, how about the picnic? I promise I'll run lines with you all day."

"I bet you will," Callie said teasingly. "In that case, you've got a deal."

"Act Two run-through," Julia called.

David stood up and held out his arm.

"Shall we, Ginger?"

"The pleasure is all mine." She laughed as she wrapped her arm in his.

"So how was the picnic?" Jennifer asked as she slammed her locker shut. "Looks like you've got a sunburn on your nose. I'm surprised you two were able to stop gazing into each other's eyes long enough to let the sun *in*."

"Very funny." Callie slapped Jennifer playfully with a notebook. "For your information, we not only had a hike and a picnic—but I managed to memorize all of Sarah's lines to perfection."

"That's not what David says," Jennifer said, teasing. "He spent most of study hall telling Mike how crazy he is about you."

"Did he really tell Mike about yesterday?"

"I was sitting right there and heard every word—not that David noticed. He's got stars for eyeballs these days."

"Oh, Jennifer, I'm so happy! You know what we're doing after the play is over? He's going to take me into New York City to see a Broadway show!"

"You're kidding! Boy, compared to David, Mike is falling down on the job. It's time to have a long talk with that guy."

"Look, I'll be late for class. See you later," Callie waved.

When she walked into the auditorium that afternoon, Callie saw Kim Crawford talking to Ken. Her veins flooded with relief and joy.

"Boy, am I glad to see *you*," Callie cried breathlessly, joining the crowd forming around Kim. "You have just saved Kennedy High from an excruciating evening and me from certain embarrassment."

"That's not what I hear." Kim smiled. "Sounds like you've been doing a great job filling in for me."

"Thanks." Callie blushed. "But it's great to have you back. I thought you were on death's door."

"No. The fever broke over the weekend. The doctor wants me to take it easy, but he thought going back to rehearsal would be the best thing for my spirits, so here I am."

"Tell me," Callie whispered, "is there any news from Ohio?"

Kim looked down at the floor. "None. Greg hasn't written, and Jane's avoiding the subject entirely," she said quietly.

Callie hugged her. "I'm sorry to hear that," she said sincerely. "I hope everything works out."

"I understand you have some good news." Kim smiled and nodded toward David, who was making his way toward them. "Julia called to tell me—I think she expected it to destroy me." She laughed.

He came up and put his arm around Callie. "Kim! Welcome back!"

"Thanks, David. It's great to be here. We've got a lot of lost time to make up for."

"We sure do. Don't worry. I know you can do it. I've got to go backstage and see Howie. Catch you later." He kissed Callie on the nose and hopped onto the stage.

"You look like you couldn't be happier," Kim said and sighed.

"We couldn't," Callie agreed, watching David as he retreated behind the curtain. "No way."

The next couple of days sped by like minutes until the first performance was upon them. Callie sat in front of her mirror in the dressing room carefully applying base with a sponge. Jennifer was next to her, fumbling with a tube of eyeliner.

"I just don't know why we have to use this gunk," Jennifer said, fuming. "It runs all over the place."

"It won't run if you just put a little on your brush, like this," Callie explained. "If you don't wear eyeliner, your eyes will disappear under the lights. Let me put it on you."

Julia stuck her head in the door.

"Forty minutes till curtain, everybody. Warm-ups in ten."

"I wonder if she barges in on the boys like that?" Angela mused.

"Argggh! I'll never be ready in time," Jennifer said excitedly.

"Of course you will, silly. And you're not even on till the third scene, so don't worry," Callie said reassuringly.

"I can't get over you! You act like you're getting ready to watch television. Aren't you the least bit nervous?"

"Jennifer, I'm a wreck. Just feel that pulse. So shut up, because you're making it worse. Would you hold still? You're going to look like something out of Kiss if you don't stop fidgeting while I put this on you."

"So how come you seem calm?"

"David says it's very important to take these opening night jitters and channel them into positive energy—you know, make them work *for* you instead of against you. I'm trying very hard to do that, but if you don't knock it off, I swear I'll fall apart right here."

"David says this, David says that—what's gotten into you?"

"Did I tell you he said he loves me?" Callie beamed.

"Only about ten times." Jennifer laughed. "But I can't remember the last time you were this happy. Love seems to agree with you."

"It's not just David, Jennifer. It's the play, it's *everything.* It seems like my whole life is falling into place at once. I just wish—"

"What could you possibly have to complain about?"

"I just wish Hattie were happier, that she could make some friends at Rosedale and not rely on me so much," Callie mused. "I love the time I spend with her, and now that rehearsals are over, I'll be able to visit more often. But she should have more to look forward to than just me."

"What about that man you told me about— Ray?"

"Roy. I don't know. She always gets mad at him."

"Probably the more he badgers her, the sooner she'll give in and admit she likes him," Jennifer suggested hopefully.

"Maybe you're right, Jen. I wish she could see me playing Adelaide. We talked about it so much, and then Kim got sick—"

"That *is* terrible," Jennifer agreed. "Maybe you can go over next week and give a command performance."

"Oh, sure—any more bright ideas?" Callie laughed.

The door swung open, and Julia bounced in again. "I hope you're decent, because the guys are about to join us for warm-ups."

"Bring 'em on!" somebody shouted.

Everyone gathered in the hall.

"Final pep talk, kids, although at this point I know you probably won't hear a word I say." Ken's words were greeted by shouts and whistles.

"Calm down," he said and laughed. "We've all worked very hard, and I think we've got a great show. Just swallow your nerves and go out there and give it all you've got. And don't forget to smile."

David, who had joined Callie, squeezed her hand and smiled down at her.

"*And*," Ken continued, "we will maintain our time-honored Kennedy tradition—the first three people to blow lines get to clean up the dressing rooms after the show." The cast hissed and booed at Ken.

"OK, everybody—let's warm up!"

Afterward, David turned to Callie and held her hands.

"Don't kiss me," she said. "You'll mess up our makeup."

"You don't know what you ask." He grinned,

then hugged her so hard she thought her ribs would crack.

"And just don't kiss Kim on stage like you kiss me," she said teasingly, "or you won't be able to go on tomorrow night."

"You know you're the only one for me," he said gently. "Break a leg, Ginger."

"Break a leg, uh, Fred. I don't know, Fred doesn't seem to suit you."

"I want David to be the only one who suits you," he said, breaking the rules and kissing her first softly and then more romantically. "I'll see you during intermission." He turned and went back to the boys' room.

Callie wrapped her arms around herself, savoring the warmth of David's hug. Then she took a deep breath and went to put on her costume.

As the curtain fell on the final act, thunderous applause erupted from the audience, and squeals of delight could be heard backstage. Julia hissed for silence and places for curtain calls. Callie waited breathlessly in the wings until it was time for her to step out and take her bow.

As the audience roared, she lowered her head. Her eye caught something glittering in the front row. It was the arm of a wheelchair, and Hattie was sitting in it, waving her program wildly. Callie's face broke into a broad smile as she noticed that Roy was by Hattie's side.

Callie stepped to her side of the stage, the applause ringing in her ears. Then David walked out, and the audience was on its feet. He acknowledged it with a bow and then winked at Callie, taking his place beside her. Kim walked out, bowed, and the curtain fell.

David turned to Callie, picked her up, and swung her around, pressing his lips to hers. "Go get dressed, Ginger—we have a cast party to go to and hordes of adoring fans out there waiting to greet us." He smiled down at her.

"Oh, David." Burying her face in his shoulder, she started to sob. He lifted her face, forcing her to look at him.

"Why are you crying, Callie?" he asked.

"I'm crying because I'm *happy*, you jerk." She started to laugh and cry at the same time.

"You're silly," he said affectionately. "What's going on here?" he said, looking around. "Kim is crying. So is Jennifer. I don't know if I can stand all this happiness."

"I'll see you in fifteen minutes. I'm going to change and get this stuff off my face."

Callie floated all the way to the dressing

room. In record time she hung up her costume, pulled on her jeans, and washed up. She was packing her things when Jennifer came in.

"Look at you, dressed already. Too bad they can't bottle happiness." Jennifer said, joking.

"I'm in a rush, Jen. See you at the cast party."

As Callie rounded the corner in the hallway, she ran headlong into Hattie and Roy, who were both grinning from ear to ear.

"Hot dog!" Hattie cried. "You were terrific!"

"Yup, you sure were," Roy agreed.

"Aw, shush, Roy. This here's my girl you're talking to." But Hattie's reprimand was good-natured, and Callie could see that Roy was definitely enjoying it.

"I can't believe you're here!" Callie beamed. "I wanted to jump right into your lap when I saw you during the curtain call."

"Do you think I would sit home while you were giving a new meaning to the word stardom? After all, I've got a bigger stake in this than anyone. Are your parents here?"

"No, they're coming tomorrow night," Callie said. "Dad's out of town on business."

Roy patted Hattie's arm and pointed to the package on her lap.

"OK, OK, I'm getting to it. Hold your horses!"

Sheepishly she turned to Callie. "Uh, here—this is for you."

Callie eagerly ripped open the paper to discover a pink carnation. She flung her arms around the old woman and kissed her.

"A-hem," came a voice from behind. "I thought that was my department," David said.

"David, this is Hattie. Remember I told you about her?" Callie said excitedly. "And this is Roy Aarons, *her friend.*" Callie shot a triumphant look at the woman in the wheelchair, who grinned back.

"I've been waiting a long time to meet you, Mrs. Stevens," David said, shaking her hand. "Callie never stops talking about you."

"Likewise." Hattie said and winked, and soon the four of them were talking and laughing.

"I think Mr. Stern must be outside with the car by now, Hattie," Roy interjected. "We don't want to keep him waiting."

"Aw, that old bat can wait—"

"*And* we don't want to keep the young people from their plans," he added firmly.

"We'll walk you to the door," Callie said, breathless.

"Home, James," Hattie instructed.

When they had seen the old couple safely

into Mr. Stern's car, they turned to go to the parking lot.

"Callie and David. Over here!" a voice called. "There's somebody I want you to meet." They turned and saw Kim holding hands with a guy they'd never seen before. Instantly Callie knew who he was.

"This is Greg Roberts, a friend from Ohio." Kim looked ecstatic.

"It's nice to meet you," Callie said, shaking his hand.

"You came all the way from Ohio to see the show?" David asked.

"Not just the show." Greg looked at Kim and smiled.

"Do you believe it?" Kim sighed happily. "Greg surprised me! My parents smuggled him from the airport after I left the house this evening."

"Do you guys have a ride to the cast party?" David asked.

"I've got the family car," Kim replied. "But don't look for us too soon. We might take the long way there." Greg hugged Kim hard.

Callie and David strolled arm and arm into the parking lot.

"Just look at those stars," Callie said dreamily.

"Hey, David!" yelled Richard Sanders from

the door. "Can we catch a ride to the cast party with you guys?"

David looked down at Callie. "I think Greg and Kim have the right idea," he whispered. "Sorry, Rich," he yelled back. "Our car's full. See you there.

"C'mon, Ginger, I'll waltz you to the car." He scooped her up in his strong arms and circled her around until they hit the fender.

As Callie opened her eyes, she saw a bouquet of white roses on the front seat. "Oh, David," she said, fresh tears starting to fall.

"Shhh," he said, putting his finger to her lips. "We don't want to wake up the flowers."

They climbed into the car, and Callie ripped open the card.

"Wait," he whispered. "Let me read it to you." The card fell from his hands, and his eyes never left hers. "To Ginger—May I never have another leading lady."